AMAZON R
'LIVING IN H/

CH00823105

This book is one of the best I have read, the honesty, love, laughter and tears all captured in one brilliant read.

An excellent read ! Touching, humorous, loving, it describes what only those parents closely associated with autism go through. For those of us who are not familiar with autism, it was an eye-opener in showing the stresses and strains, but also the love and rewards that can come with it.

It is full of honesty, humour but most of all love and respect with seemingly getting little in return. Everyone should read this book, whether touched by autism or not. It would help to make us all more tolerant and accepting of those that are a little bit different.

I loved this book! As a parent of two autistic people myself, I can assure would be readers that the life described by Denis Deasy in this entertaining tale is spot on!

AMAZON REVIEWS FOR
'I'M SORRY, MY SON'S AUTISTIC'

What an amazing follow up to 'Living in Harry's World' joining Harry and his dad on a heart-warming but rollercoaster of a ride into adulthood. The author really opened my eyes to the world of autism and is a very humbling read. Fantastic read that I couldn't put down. I can't wait until the next instalment.

Author Denis Deasy brilliantly conveys the pressures of dealing with stressful behavioural issues by injecting a degree of humour which is not only entertaining but also gives the reader some insights into the realities of living with autism. I laughed out loud at times and had a tear in my eye at others. This follow-up is highly recommended.

The relationship between Harry and his father is so moving. I loved the many funny incidents and anecdotes - based on Harry's view of the world. A very honest, yet uplifting, account of life with an autistic teenager.

AMAZON REVIEWS FOR 'FROM THIS DAY FORWARD'

The final part of the trilogy from author Denis Deasy concludes the story arc of autistic Harry and his long suffering father. Beautifully written, we see Harry at 30 in a relationship and planning to marry Bernadette. Just like the previous two books in the series, you'll laugh out loud at some parts and will have tears in your eyes at others. Books like this really do give an insight into life with autism but few do it as well as Deasy.

The completion of the 'Harry' trilogy and the best yet? Charming, insightful and full of humour. These books have offered real insight into families living with autism and yet manage to both entertain and educate the casual reader. Highly recommended!

Having read this third book about Harry, getting more insight into the world of an autistic person, the heartache, and sometimes joy, of the parents involved, I am still in awe, and have full respect for them, for dealing with, and working through a life-long commitment.

AMAZON REVIEWS FOR 'DON'T LICK THE MAILBOX'

This is the author's fourth novel dealing with autism. The previous three form the 'Harry' trilogy which shone a bright light on the condition through characters both directly and constantly engaged with it. In Don't Lick the Mailbox, Denis Deasy takes a different approach to the subject as the main character, IT professional Danny, unwittingly meets autism head on with no previous knowledge or experience. The result is another insightful and entertaining read; a journey into a challenging world that expertly charts the numerous highs and lows with keenly-observed drama and humour.

A beautifully written book about the world of autism from the perspective of a teenager. This is a topic I know little about but after finishing the book, I felt I had a better understanding of the challenges some people have to deal with. Written with charm, humour and soul this is touching story that could easily be made into a BBC drama.

A great read and a fascinating and eye opening insight into the world of autistic parenting.

He'll Eat the Head off Ya

Denis Deasy

Grosvenor House
Publishing Limited

This book is published by
Grosvenor House Publishing Ltd
Link House
140 The Broadway, Tolworth, Surrey, KT6 7HT.
www.grosvenorhousepublishing.co.uk

This book is a work of fiction. Any resemblance to
people or events, past or present, is purely coincidental.

A CIP record for this book
is available from the British Library

ISBN 978-1-80381-606-7
eBook ISBN 978-1-80381-607-4

deasy85@ntlworld.com

DEDICATION

This book is dedicated to my friend, Sean Poole.
I cannot tell you how much your enthusiasm
and positive feedback has helped me when
I have doubts about my work.

ACKNOWLEDGEMENTS

Writing a book is not easy, in fact it's very hard but I am lucky that I can call on Sean Poole, Tony Prouse and Joanna Rees. Their respective talents have helped me immensely and for that I am extremely grateful.

My wife, Joanmarie, drew the book cover and I absolutely love it. I am thrilled that you are taking up art again. The two men on the cover are actually my sons, Denis and James. This book really is a family effort.

Thanks to my mum and my Irish cousin, Denis Deasy, (my namesake) for the book title.

Last but not least are my publishers, Grosvenor House. Self-publishing can be a daunting prospect but they make everything seem so easy and do such a beautiful job. They are just the best.

CHAPTER ONE:
SIENNA

'Doesn't my mum love me anymore?' Kieran asks.

'Of course she does. Why do you say that?' I reply.

'She normally comes on the third Saturday of the month but she's not here.'

'She's just moved to Blackburn to be with her partner. We've been through this.'

'Where the hell's that shithole?'

'It's in the north, over a four hour drive from here.'

'Does that mean I'll never see her again?'

'No but her visiting times will be different, as she's so far away.'

'So who's going to visit me instead?'

I'm struggling to find the right response.

'Doesn't she like me anymore?' He asks.

'Of course she does, she loves you. Please don't worry about that.'

'Do all Mums move four hours away from their children when they get fed up?'

'I'll tell you what, let's go for a walk to the shops. We can get a KitKat if you want?' I say, in an attempt to deflect him from this line of conversation.

'OK, I just love KitKats.'

Kieran is a twenty-seven year old autistic man. He's a resident in a special needs care home called StarLight, which is a five minute walk from Finsbury Park tube station in London. Kieran has been at StarLight since he was twenty-one. There are three other adult residents here, all male and autistic.

I'm Sienna and I've been Kieran's sole carer for the last three years. We get along really well most of the time although our relationship wasn't always this smooth. When I joined here I came with all the necessary academic qualifications but that did not prepare me in any way for Kieran.

His previous carer was sacked after she slapped Kieran across his face in an angry confrontation with him. She immediately realised that she made a big mistake and apologised but her fate was sealed. This happened before I joined and from what my work colleagues told me she was usually a calm person but dealing with Kieran at that time was extremely stressful and she was obviously pushed to the limit.

After my first few weeks with Kieran I was on the verge of quitting. He was an angry young man and hostile to me. Everything and nothing triggered his fury. On numerous occasions he would throw his dinner plate against the wall, usually smashing the plate, all because his fish fingers weren't positioned in the way that he had anticipated or the beans were touching his chips. Preparing his meal was extremely stressful.

He would constantly spit at me, sometimes because I was smiling too much or he didn't like the way I had my hair in a ponytail. It was a steep learning curve.

All the other adults in the home had their own behavioural issues but none were as aggressive as Kieran.

His greeting to me every morning for the past three years has always been the same - 'morning, dildo.' I've no idea where this originates from. I asked him if he knew what a dildo was and he told me 'it's a plastic for whores.' I never pushed him further.

It took me nearly six months before he began to trust me or at least stop the spitting.

So why did I stick it out for six months when I could so easily have transferred to another home? I saw a sadness in him and it broke my heart. His worried expression never left him and it's still there.

His parents split up when he was twelve. His father had an affair and from my understanding moved to Devon with the woman. His father has never visited him in all the time I've been here and Kieran doesn't get any birthday or Christmas cards from him, let alone any presents.

His mother, Sally, is a good person. She did her best bringing up her son but as he got older she found it increasingly difficult. At sixteen Kieran was in his first care home but he didn't stay there too long due to his disruptive behaviour. He attended two other care homes before joining StarLight.

When Sally comes, she takes him out for a meal or a bit of shopping but she's usually back within three hours, never longer.

Three hours a month equates to thirty-six hours a year. Kieran needs more than a day and a half with his mother but that's all she can manage. She simply can't cope.

He usually spits at her when she arrives. Is that because he resents the lack of time with his mother? I sometimes ask him why he does that and he just tells me 'I like to see my spittle covering her face.'

Sometimes Sally comes back to the house after only half an hour. It's no wonder Kieran looks permanently troubled.

But there's another member of the family that I've never seen and that's Kieran's brother, Ryan. From my brief conversations with Sally she told me that Ryan is three years older than Kieran and left home when he was sixteen. I believe that Ryan hasn't seen his brother since the day he left. However, unlike his father, he does send Kieran birthday and Christmas cards, and presents too. In fact, yesterday I asked Kieran whether he'd like to see Ryan again but he just replied 'he vanished from me.'

So I will take Kieran out to get his KitKat and hopefully that will distract him from his thoughts about his mother.

As Sally now lives in Blackburn I fear she will now fall short of her yearly thirty-six hours visiting time.

CHAPTER TWO:
SIENNA

After my conversation with Kieran I ring Sally.

'Can I ask you a personal question?' I inquire.

'Yeah, go ahead.'

'I had a chat with Kieran earlier and Ryan's name came up. How about I try to contact Ryan to see if he wants to meet Kieran?'

'I don't think that's a good idea.'

'Why not?'

'Because of Kieran's issues growing up all of our attention was naturally focused on him at the expense of Ryan and he resented us all for it. As he got older Ryan started to mix with the wrong crowd and got into trouble with the police a few times, mainly nicking stuff from shops, which meant he had to do community service a couple of times. I tried to reach out to him but he wasn't interested. However he does write to me every Christmas just to let me know that he's doing OK but doesn't give me any details. The last address I had for him was in Kings Cross. It's obvious he doesn't want anything to do with me or Kieran, and certainly not his father.'

'Can I just try? What have we got to lose? I won't tell Kieran unless Ryan agrees to meet up. With you being so far away I think Kieran's lonely. I really believe it's worth pursuing but obviously I won't do anything unless you agree to it.'

'But what if Ryan does want to see his brother and they simply don't get on? It'll open up old wounds. Wouldn't that upset Kieran even more?'

'Yes, of course it's a risk but if I could meet up with Ryan I'll get a good idea of what's he like right now and will make a decision based on that. If there's any doubt in my mind that it might go pear shaped I'll drop it.'

'How did Ryan's name crop up in the first place? Kieran hasn't talked about him for years.'

'He's anxious that your visits will be less frequent and actually questioned whether anyone will ever visit him, so it was me that mentioned Ryan.'

'And what was his reaction?'

'He just said that Ryan vanished. Ryan's probably no longer living at that address so it might all come to nothing but isn't it worth finding out if there's any possibility that he might reconnect with his brother again? From what you told me Ryan didn't sound like a bad person, he just went off the rails and to some extent you can understand that, but he's older now and hopefully wiser. Don't you want to have Ryan back in your life?'

'Don't you think I've tried? Not once has he given me the slightest indication that he wanted to meet up again so why do you think that you'll succeed where I've clearly failed?'

'Maybe the fact that I'm coming at it from an outsiders' point of view might help?'

'Please, please don't tell Kieran your intentions until you know that it's going to happen. God knows he's been through enough shit in his short life already.'

'Of course, does that mean I can go ahead?'

'Yes, but keep me informed every step of the way.'

CHAPTER THREE:
SIENNA

Have I opened up a can of worms? If I do get in contact with Ryan I've got to be absolutely convinced that he's not going to upset Kieran even if he does want to meet up with him. The last thing I need is for Kieran to revert back to his aggressive behaviours. I feel under intense pressure already but what's the alternative? Do nothing? Sally is Kieran's only visitor. I believe there are other relatives but I remember Sally telling me that whenever there were any family gatherings the nieces and nephews stayed away from Kieran. They found him too strange. Naturally this upset Sally and consequently she avoided future family occasions to the point where she wasn't invited anymore. In a nutshell Kieran, and by default Sally, were being punished for his autism. So Ryan is my only hope.

I've asked Sally about Ryan a few times previously but the mere mention of his name seemed to upset her so I never pursued it, until now.

This is so risky and has to be handled very carefully.

As I approach StarLight on this cold, frosty morning I glance at my surroundings. It's a quiet, residential street, although the Arsenal football club stadium is only a five minute walk away and whenever Arsenal are playing thousands of spectators walk right past StarLight. The noise they make upsets some of our residents so on match days we tend to take them out somewhere to avoid this. This may involve going swimming, ten pin bowling, trampolining etc. The StarLight building was built in Victorian times and is just beautiful. It has three floors, tall ceilings and a beautiful garden at the back. The houses on either side of us are the same and the owners are just wonderful. Living next door to a house of four special needs adults can't be easy. One of the neighbours is Eve and she often bakes cakes for our residents.

'Michael McIntyre's a nice man,' Jamie tells me, before I have a chance to take my coat off.

Jamie is one of the residents.

'Yes, he seems to be.'

'He's only five foot seven and I'm six foot one so I could easily head-butt him.'

'Well you don't want to do that, do you?'

'Not all the time, because he makes me laugh. But when he tells a shit joke I think he needs a head-butt to get him back on track. Anyway I'd like him to visit me.'

'He's a busy man.'

'But nobody comes here so if he did I'll be the happiest person ever. I bet his wife laughs from the moment she wakes up to when she goes to bed. She's so lucky being his wife when all she has to do is laugh.'

I'm going to do my best to get a fan mail contact for Michael McIntyre and ask for a signed photo. Jamie's right when he says that he doesn't get any visitors. His parents are still together as far as I know but I've never seen them. How can they just abandon their only son? I just don't understand it at all. This seems to be a common theme.

'McIntyre always looks so smart in his suit. I've never worn a suit,' Jamie informs me.

I make a mental note to get him a suit for Christmas. Our 'home' gives each resident a Christmas present but it's usually something like a ten pound *Amazon* voucher so I try to get them a more personal gift and I don't mind splashing out a bit. They all deserve it.

Kieran joins us.

'So what are we doing today? Can we go and watch Arsenal play? They're playing West Ham and that lot can't kick a ball straight. They always kick it into the crowd instead of the goal. They're all simpletons.'

I don't remember Gary Lineker ever referring to a team as simpletons or saying that they can't kick a ball straight so maybe there's a vacancy on *Match Of The Day* for another football pundit. The alternative view.

'All the tickets are sold out but we can watch it on *Sky*.'

'Nah, I don't like those commentators prattling on and on about bullshit.'

'Just turn the sound down.'

'But then it's too quiet.'

The last time I took Kieran to Arsenal we visited a chip shop near the stadium and Kieran got his usual sausage and chips, which he loved. He then told me he was full up and happy so he wanted to go straight back home instead of watching the game. Oh well, those tickets only cost forty-five pounds each.

'Anyway, where's that bloke who used to come and pick you up in his car?' Kieran asks me. 'I haven't seen him for twenty-seven days. You know, the bloke with long legs and little hair in his eyebrows.'

'Philip and me split up a couple of weeks ago.'

'Was it because of his eyebrows?'

'No, it had nothing to do with his eyebrows.'

'Because he had long legs and you've got short legs did he get a backache when he tried to kiss you and then just left you because he wanted his back to get better?'

'No, his back was fine.'

'Was it because you slurp when you drink?'

I smile at his comment but shake my head.

'Or was it because your cooking is a bit shit?'

'No, it was because we didn't love each other anymore.'

'I'm glad because he always beeped his car horn when he came to pick you up and when you didn't come out straight away he kept on beeping it. He was a noisy arsehole in his car.'

Kieran's got a point. That car beeping was really irritating but that wasn't the reason why we split up and it wasn't because of his plucked eyebrows or my short legs or my slurping or indeed my suspect cooking ability. Philip told me that it was all to do with my job. He said it took over my life and he was probably right but he never understood why I loved my job so much. He's a lawyer and naturally earns good money and felt with my qualifications I could do much better than looking after special needs adults. Whilst he didn't come right out and say that, his attitude and subtle dismissal of my job made it obvious how he felt.

I've always wanted to be a carer for special needs children or adults. I have a severely autistic cousin called Adam who's the same age as me – twenty-six - and I saw first-hand how his extended family and the public at large treated him. They barely paid any attention to him because he's completely non-verbal. To some extent I could understand that from his peers when he was growing up. Children need interaction and feedback and Adam couldn't provide that, not in the way they wanted anyway but adults would barely acknowledge him in family get-togethers and that broke my heart. His parents, aunt Cara and uncle Tim, are just wonderful with Adam. He's their only child and they adore him. Luckily they've always lived near me and I've been visiting Adam since I was a little girl. I progressed from playing with him to taking him shopping with me at weekends. Philip only met Adam once and that encounter was awkward. He didn't know what to say to Adam, which to some extent I understood but I knew he wasn't interested. Philip actually ended our relationship, saying that we had drifted apart and wanted different things in life. As it was only a couple of weeks ago I'm still hurting. Despite his lack of understanding over my job situation I thought we got along quite well, even though in the past couple of months our relationship was strained. We saw less of each other due to our work commitments.

He always wanted to socialise – whether it's going to expensive restaurants, VIP boxes at football stadiums or pub crawls with his work colleagues, most of whom I've nothing in common with. He never understood why I had to stay at work longer than normal to make sure that Kieran was OK after an unsettling day, rather than attend some highfalutin event with him

Will the demands of my job have an impact on any future relationships? Only time will tell.

But my thoughts turn to Ryan. He lives two stops on the tube from the care home and it's on my way home so I'm going to find out if he's still at the address that Sally gave me and if so will he agree to see his brother after leaving home over fourteen years ago.

CHAPTER FOUR:
SIENNA

I'm standing outside what I hope is Ryan's flat and I'm feeling tense. Am I doing the right thing? What would be the worst case scenario if I walk away now? Sally will probably be relieved and Kieran will be none the wiser. It's the safer option but Kieran has only his mother and no friends, apart from some of his fellow residents, so wouldn't his life be enriched if he got together with his brother? It's got to be worth the risk, so I ring the bell.

The man at the door is definitely Ryan. He's much taller than Kieran but he has the same eyes, hair colour and stance as his brother.

I've found him.

'Can I help you?' He asks, sounding a little pissed off.

'Are you Ryan Doyle?'

'Who's asking?'

'My name's Sienna. I work at StarLight and I'm Kieran's carer.'

'Is he OK?' He asks, looking anxious.

'Yes, he's doing fine. I'm sorry, I didn't mean to scare you. I just wanted to have a chat.'

'About what?'

'I'm not sure if you're aware but your mother has just moved to Blackburn...'

I'm anticipating an acknowledgement but there's none.

'And consequently she'll find it more difficult to visit Kieran and I wondered if we could discuss the possibility of you seeing him.'

'Did my mum put you up to this?'

'No, not at all. But I did ask her if it was OK to talk to you and she agreed to it.'

'No can do. I've got my own life now and I'm happy with it so thanks for looking after my brother and I'm sorry it was a wasted journey for you.'

'Please can I just have a few minutes of your time? Don't you want to hear how Kieran's getting on? I've brought some recent photos of him. You haven't seen him in such a long time and he'd be thrilled to see you again.'

'I'm sorry...'

With that he shuts the door. I ring the bell several more times but he doesn't respond. Well that didn't go as well as I would've liked but what were my expectations? Did I really think that he was going to break down and declare his undying love for his brother and proclaim his regrets for not seeing him when he so clearly blames Kieran for all the troubles in his life? But I hoped against hope that I could've had a chat with him to bring him up to date with everything that has happened to Kieran since they last were together.

Family setups are all so complicated. If I had a special needs brother I would find it unthinkable to exclude him from my life but I know from witnessing the fractured family circumstances at StarLight that the Doyle family set up is unfortunately very common, so maybe I'm in the minority.

I take a handful of photos and push them through Ryan's letterbox. I wait a few minutes but there's no reaction so I reluctantly make my way back to Kings Cross tube station.

CHAPTER FIVE: RYAN

From my bedroom window I see the pretty lady walk away. I thought that she was going to camp out there all night.

What the hell just happened? My hands are shaking. I need a drink and fast. I pour myself a nice cold glass of wine.

What was her name again? I think she said Sienna but our conversation is all a bit of a blur right now. She seems like a nice person and I'm glad that she's looking after my brother but I felt her visit was intrusive. Is it the correct procedure to simply turn up at my flat unannounced?

I knew that Mum was dating a guy from up north but I had no idea it was that serious. However, my lack of knowledge is all down to me as I've made it quite clear that I don't want anything to do with my family. Everything that has gone wrong in my life has been associated with my parents and my brother.

I was fifteen when I first started going to pubs and one night I saw my father kissing another woman and touching her inappropriately. He didn't notice me as I left straight away but when I confronted him a few days later he told me in no uncertain terms that I wasn't to say anything to Mum. He tried to play it down by saying that he was a little drunk and just having a bit of fun but I knew he was lying. I never did tell Mum and I regret that.

My relationship with my father was always been strained. He rarely showed any affection towards Kieran or me. He never seemed to be around much, not through work, mostly out in the pub with his mates or his female acquaintances. I saw him several more times in pubs with various ladies and even when he saw me he never acknowledged my presence and just carried on as if I wasn't there.

The happy, chatty person that I witnessed in the pub was a million miles away from the cold and distant man who lived with us.

He's an evil man and I hate him.

Growing up with Kieran was extremely stressful. I do clearly remember that from a very early age he rarely slept much at night and the stress it caused my parents, particularly my mother. When he was really young he'd wake up at around one o'clock in the morning. Mum wanted to bring him into their bed but Dad refused. I remember hearing them argue so many times about who would look after him as Kieran would often wander downstairs looking for goodies. He just couldn't be left to his own devices even when he grew older. It was nearly always Mum who either had to lay down with Kieran in his own bed or more often than not go downstairs with him. Dad rarely did this. He would often say to Mum – 'you do fuck all during the day so you can catch up with your sleep when he has a kip.' The problem was Kieran could survive on only a few hours' sleep, it never seemed to catch up with him so it was rare that he needed any extra 'kip'.

This sleeping pattern continued until I left home.

As Kieran got older he developed some bizarre behavioural traits. At four years old he was still in nappies and he would smear his excrement all over the house, on the sofa, TV, my toys – you name it he smeared it. He would constantly pinch me and Mum would get extremely angry with me if I retaliated. 'But he hit me' I would say to her but her reply was always 'he can't help it.' Whenever I complained to Mum she would always defend him no matter what he did to me. I cannot ever remembering hitting him back, my retaliation was verbal – 'you're a fucking simpleton', 'why can't you be normal?', 'I hate you,' – quite cruel but I am amazed that I didn't attack him, maybe I knew that he couldn't help his actions. Also, Mum was nearly always with him so the opportunity to hit back was never an option.

As he got older the aggression towards me got more intense and this was almost always without any provocation.

Kieran would spit at me and Mum the first thing in the morning and bite my hair every day. I was a nervous wreck around him.

When he was five he was diagnosed as autistic. I didn't know what the hell that was and when I asked my father he just replied 'he's mental.'

Mum was so wrapped up with Kieran's issues that she rarely had any time for me. She was always short tempered whenever I asked her something. On reflection this was probably due to her lack of sleep and of course dealing with all of Kieran's problems, but at the time I had no idea why she was so cruel. Sometimes I'd ask her for help with my homework but her reply was always 'go and see Dad', knowing full well that was a waste of time. My father was always doing something far more important than paying any attention to me.

At times I felt sorry for my mum but why the hell did she marry that arsehole? Why didn't she know that he was an absolute prick at the beginning of their relationship?

Sometimes when I've had a few drinks I reflect on my upbringing and I try to analyse my mother's role in all of this. Kieran's issues completely took over her life and it got to the stage that I was simply left alone most of the time. She would make my breakfast and dinner and would occasionally ask how I was getting on at school but our conversations were few and far between. Consequently my school work suffered and I started to hate Kieran more and more.

My life was a misery and I couldn't wait to get out of that house. I left school with one GCSE and managed to get a job at KFC, which earned me just enough to rent a grotty one bedroom flat just off the Caledonian Road in North London. Although the area was shit, full of gangs and drug addicts, I was delighted to be living on my own. Mum was surprised when I told her I was leaving but didn't try to stop me, Dad couldn't care less. Kieran just kept staring at me on the day I left. I often wonder what he was thinking at the time?

In the weeks and months that followed I did think about my family but as time moved on these thoughts became less and less. I was enjoying my freedom even though it did lead me into a lot of trouble.

I pour myself another glass of wine and pick up the photos that Sienna put through my letterbox.

I spend ages just staring at these photos with tears rolling down my face, as I see my brother as an adult for the very first time.

CHAPTER SIX:
SIENNA

Kieran, Jamie and Billy are all waiting for me as I enter the recreation room.

Twice a week we discuss various topics and today it is how not to insult people. This may seem like a Monty Python sketch but it's something that they all need guidance on.

'Morning, dildo,' Kieran proclaims.

This could be an excellent starting point but do I really want to spend the morning talking about dildos? I think not.

'So when was the last time any of you insulted someone?' I ask them.

They all stare at me and say nothing.

'Let's start with you, Kieran. You said something quite rude to me yesterday, didn't you?'

Kieran shakes his head.

'You actually asked me when was the last time I had sex.'

'What's wrong with that?'

'That's very personal and intrusive.'

'When we went to Sainsbury's on Saturday I asked the cashier lady that question.'

'And what did she say?'

'She said I was rude but I told her that she didn't have to give me the exact time, just the date would be fine.'

'And now did she react to that?'

'She stared at me and then she noticed my 'I have AUTISM please be patient' badge and just smiled at me, but she still didn't answer my question.'

That badge is extremely helpful when dealing with the public but it seemingly comes with special powers as the owner of it can say what the hell he/she likes to anyone without any repercussions.

'OK, I think we've exhausted this subject but can you stop asking people about their sexual habits?'

'But it's my favourite part of the day.'

'Billy, did you offend anyone recently?'

'I said good morning to you yesterday.'

'But that's a nice thing to say.'

'I was nervous because you looked a bit of a mess, your hair was all over the place. You actually looked pathetic so it was probably a bad morning for you.'

'Now that's exactly what I'm talking about. You just said I looked pathetic. Even if I do look pathetic you shouldn't say it because it's hurtful.'

'I'm just telling the truth.'

'But sometimes you've got to keep your thoughts to yourself if they are negative about someone else. Do you understand?'

'No.'

'Just because you think I look pathetic don't tell me that, pay me a compliment instead.'

'Like what?'

'How about admiring the jumper I'm wearing?'

'I can't do that.'

'Why?'

'It's crap. Take it back to the shop and buy some crisps instead.'

'But I like my jumper otherwise I wouldn't wear it.'

'Then maybe you've gone a bit mad.'

It does feel like I'm fighting a losing battle but I've got to persevere.

'Just say nice things to people and keep all the negative thoughts to yourself.'

'So I have to keep all my bad thoughts, like your jumper and your pathetic expression, stored in my brain forever and only speak to people about my good thoughts?'

'Yes, that's it. Anyway, what about you, Jamie? Can you tell me what happened at Costa Coffee last week?'

'I had a lovely blueberry muffin.'

'What about when you told that woman that she looks like a fat elephant? That wasn't very nice was it?'

'Her fatness pissed me off because she was blocking my view of all the muffins, so when the cashier asked me what I wanted to eat, I asked the elephant monster to move her flabby arse out of the way.'

'And of course she didn't like that, did she?'

'Well she shouldn't have a fat arse then should she? It's all her fault.'

'In future if you see a man or woman that may a bit overweight just don't mention it to them and if you have to ask them to move so you can look at the muffins don't make any reference to any part of their body, especially their posterior.'

Jamie just shrugs his shoulders.

One of the common behavioural traits in autism is a lack of empathy. So by Jamie telling the woman that she looks like an elephant and has a fat arse he doesn't mean to cause offence. He simply doesn't understand how the woman could be hurt by these remarks. He's just verbalising what he's thinking without taking anything else into consideration. Can you imagine if we all did this?

If a child or adult misbehaves and gets told off by an authoritative figure sooner or later the penny will drop in most cases. For an autistic child or adult this requires repeating the same thing over and over and over again in the hope that it will sink in.

Teaching autistic adults is a massive challenge but when something clicks with them it's so rewarding. Sometimes it brings me to tears.

We continue this discussion for a couple more hours before we take a lunch break. I take my sandwich and Coke to the StarLight garden. My thoughts immediately turn to my brief encounter with Ryan. I was so disappointed that he didn't give me the opportunity to discuss the matter with him. I had hoped that after seeing Kieran's photos he might have had a change of heart, but apparently not. There will be no emotional reunion. Sally doesn't know that I went to Ryan's yesterday so I'll call her after work.

On the other side of the garden I see my colleague, Mandy, with Nicky. He is twenty-nine years old and severely autistic. Like my cousin, Adam, he is completely non-verbal. He's more aggressive than Adam and probably the most troubled of all the residents. I just can't imagine how he could go through life without uttering one word? That frustration must partially account for his destructive behaviour.

I approach them.

'So how are you today, Nicky?' I ask, using Makaton sign language, which is used extensively for autistic children and adults.

Nicky grits his teeth and bangs his head with his fist. There is a huge bump on his forehead because of this. It's always been there. When he gets really angry he smashes his head a number of times on walls or floors and one of the carers will usually get a punch or a head butt when we attempt to stop him from doing this.

'I gave him a ham and tomato sandwich which he obviously didn't like so he threw it into Eve's garden. At least her dog will have a nice lunch,' Mandy says.

Nicky hits his head a lot. Because of his severe autism he finds it hard to communicate. This can include things like making sense of your own feelings, communicating how you feel and interacting and socialising with others. These challenges can mean you are more likely to experience anxiety and depression, which may make you more vulnerable to self-harm.

Nicky's needs are primal. He has no interest in watching TV, reading a book or playing sports, his obsession is food. When we're preparing a meal he gets both very excited and agitated. If there's any sort of a delay in getting that dinner onto his plate he will often lash out at whoever the cook is. This would usually result in a kick in the shins, a punch to the face, a head butt or a hefty pinch in the arm. After he eventually calms down he then wants to apologise by attempting to kiss his victim and he won't settle down until the injured party has reciprocated his kiss.

Like all the residents here, Nicky is a complicated man.

'Mandy, do you want me to take him for a walk?'

'Thanks so much, I'll keep an eye on the others.'

The camaraderie amongst carers here is priceless. We all help each other and it's needed as this job takes its toll.

'Shall we go to the shops?' I ask Nicky, making the Makaton sign, which is pushing the palms of my hands in a downward motion.

He stares at me, then takes my hand and pulls me towards the front door.

Taking Nicky out is a precarious operation. He likes to go up to members of the public which usually involves tapping them on the shoulder or stamping on their feet. He went through a short period of punching the testicles of whatever guy happened to be near him, which as you can imagine did not go down well. Luckily the testicle attacks seem to have stopped but I'm under no illusions that they may restart. The care home got a number of complaints during this period.

As we're walking towards the shops I am holding onto him tightly but he still touches everyone he passes. I try to explain his autism but only a handful react positively to my comments.

As he walks past a parked car he gives it a flick and the driver immediately gets out to inspect the damage.

'What the fuck are you doing?' He shouts at Nicky.

'I'm sorry, he's autistic. There's no damage, he just likes to hear the sound it makes,' I reply.

'Well tell him to do it to someone else's car,' he replies as he examines his car for a non-existent dent. I know that Nicky's strong but I think even Superman would struggle to make a dent with such a light touch.

'Thanks for your understanding,' I reply, hoping that he's picked up on my sarcastic tone but I don't wait to find out.

Unfortunately this is a common reaction from members of the public. Most people have very little tolerance for autism, which totally baffles me. From my experience only a handful of people would cheerfully dismiss any such encounter. Mostly I'd either get a blank stare even after my explanation or a completely unforgiving reaction.

As we're approaching WH Smiths Nicky approaches a middle-aged woman and stamps on her foot. It's not a stamp with any sort of aggression but obviously she's taken aback. I immediately apologise and tell her the well-rehearsed speech about Nicky's autism but she's not interested.

'How dare you. How would you like it if I stamped on your foot?' She yells at Nicky.

'He's completely non-verbal so he can't answer your question but he likes it when other people stamp on his foot so if it makes you feel better go ahead, fill your boots.'

She looks at us both for a couple of seconds before departing.

'Thanks for your compassion,' I shout after her.

I always apologise if any of the residents approach members of the public, regardless of the severity of the encounter but if that apology is not accepted I get extremely defensive. In fact I've had a couple of complaints made to the care home about my reaction but I really don't care. They get to experience autism for a matter of seconds – can you imagine how they could possibly cope if they had a daughter or son and had to live with it?

Rant over but it does piss me off.

We enter Sainsbury's and Nicky heads straight to the bakery aisle. He points to the Victoria Sponge cake and makes a grunting sound. This is my cue to tell him what the product is.

'Victoria Sponge cake.'

He grunts several more times and each time he does this I tell him the product name.

'Do you want to buy it?'

He shakes his head. Although he's non-verbal his understanding of simple commands is very good.

He continues to point at numerous other products throughout the store and I continue verbalising the product description of each item.

After an hour spent in the store we leave after purchasing a packet of jelly babies.

Just as we approach the care home my mobile buzzes, it's a text from Ryan.

'Apologies for my abrupt manner yesterday. Any possibility of meeting up?'

'Of course. Can I come to yours at 06:30pm?' I text back.

'Yes, that's fine.'

I enter the care home with a spring in my step.

CHAPTER SEVEN: SIENNA

'Please come in,' Ryan tells me.

He guides me into the living-room.

'Would you like a drink? Beer, wine, tea, coffee?'

'A glass of white wine would be nice, thanks.'

'No problem. Please take a seat.'

I look at my surroundings. It's a nice, tidy room; very minimalistic. There's no photos of Kieran, in fact there's no photos at all.

Ryan returns with my wine. He's drinking the same.

'So what made you change your mind?' I ask.

'I'm not sure I have but I just want to hear what you have to say,' he replies in a defensive tone.

'OK, I'll fill you in. I've been Kieran's carer for the last three years so I can give you a lot of detail for that period but I only know a brief history before then.'

'Let's start with the brief history, if you don't mind?'

'StarLight is his fourth home. From my understanding the other homes couldn't cope with him. As you already know he was extremely aggressive and would constantly hit his fellow residents for no apparent reason. He also didn't sleep much which caused a number of issues with the overnight staff.'

'Where did he stay in between the homes?'

'At your mother's and she'd be the first to admit that she struggled with him.'

'And there was I thinking that her favourite son could do no wrong? How could that be possible when he was actually a pain in the arse all this time?'

'Do you want me to carry on?' I ask more aggressively than I intended.

He nods.

'When he was eighteen he was prescribed Ritalin to calm him down.'

'Did it help?'

'From what I've read in his case history it worked for a short period but he soon regressed. They upped his medicine but again it was only briefly effective. He struggled in his first couple of years at StarLight with the same issues I've already mentioned but gradually things started to improve.'

'In what way?' He asks as he tops up his glass of wine.

'Although he's no longer on Ritalin he's less aggressive now, however he does still have his moments and when it gets really bad we have to give him a drug called Lorazepam.'

'And what does that do?'

'It relives anxiety very quickly. We only use it when he gets out of control.'

I'm anticipating another question or comment but he remains silent.

'He gets on reasonably well with the other residents now but one thing that hasn't changed is his lack of sleep. He only sleeps three to four hours a night.'

'And what does he do when he's up?'

'We try to keep him in his bedroom but if he's too noisy we bring him downstairs where he'll just watch TV.'

'Does he ever mention me?'

'Not much, but the other day I did ask him about you and he told me you just vanished.'

Ryan looks tense and just stares at the living-room wall. I don't know if that means he's feeling remorseful for missing out on so much in his brother's life or just reflecting on his own difficult family upbringing. I suspect it's the latter.

'Do you mind if I ask a personal question?' I ask.

'Go ahead.'

'Have you been in contact with your father since you left home?'

'Are you fucking kidding me?'

'I'm sorry I didn't mean to upset you…'

'He's a nasty arsehole. I don't care if he's dead or alive. He was horrible. I've no idea why Mum didn't leave him but I suppose she was busy raising us and he was the breadwinner, although he seemed to spend most of his money in the pub or on his many female acquaintances.'

'Sally told me he was unfaithful.'

'She doesn't know the half of it. I suppose I followed in his footsteps by spending too much time in the pub. At fifteen I was six foot one and looked older than I was, which enabled me to frequent some pubs without too many questions being asked. To be honest most of the local pubs didn't give a shit anyway. The reason I'm telling you this is that I saw my father in several of the pubs with various tarts and he was usually in some intimate embrace. Initially I found it shocking but I got used to seeing my pathetic father in these situations. I should've confronted him more but the few times I did he just dismissed it. He's a waste of space and he disgusts me.'

'Did you tell Sally?'

'No but I wish I had. It wouldn't have made any difference. She relied on his income.'

'When your father left did the atmosphere improve?'

'Although I always avoided being in the same room as him it was a relief knowing that he was no longer around. But my mother was stressed out all the time. She just lost her husband and from my understanding he gave her little child support so if anything the atmosphere was even more strained.'

'How did this affect Kieran?' I ask, encouraged by his openness.

'I've no idea. He just seemed to carry on as normal. This is turning into a bit of an interrogation, isn't it?'

'It'll help me deal with Kieran if I get more details on his background from your perspective. But if you're uncomfortable with this then I'll stop.'

'No, I'm sorry if I'm coming off too aggressive. It just brings back some really bad memories. Ones I've tried to block out for so many years. You're the only person that I've talked to about my past.'

'I'm going to ask even more personal questions now if that's OK? I know that life was extremely difficult for you growing up and I'm guessing that's the reason why you left so early but listening to you now you seem almost sympathetic towards your mother's situation but yet you're so resentful towards her, completely cutting her out of your life. Don't you think she was in an impossible position? Kieran's problems took over her life but that wasn't her fault.'

'Are you sure you're not a fully qualified psychologist?'

'Yes I'm sure.'

'When I was at home and Kieran's behavioural issues ruled the household my mother blocked me out of her life. Now I'm older I understand that to some degree but it wasn't just a case of ignoring me, she was nasty and short tempered towards me but showed all the patience in the world with Kieran. I'll never forgive her for that. I needed her but she just seemed to resent me for being normal.'

'OK, I understand what you're saying. How about I arrange a meeting with your mother before we even think about seeing Kieran? I know that she'll agree to it.'

'No, I'm not ready for that. Look I think we've discussed enough about my past tonight. Do you mind if we drop it for now?'

'Of course. This will probably require a few more visits, if you're agreeable to that?'

'We'll see. It's my turn to ask you something. Why are you so determined to reunite me and Kieran? What's in it for you?'

'There's no ulterior motive. There are hardly any visitors to any of our residents. I think they're lonely and that includes Kieran. I feel sorry for them, they deserve better.'

'Are you ramping up the guilt trip?' He asks.

'No, that definitely wasn't my intention.'

He looks at me but doesn't respond. I'm not sure he believes me. We talk for another hour without mentioning Kieran or Sally. When I pressed him on what he did after leaving home he revealed that after a number of casual jobs he went to college and obtained the necessary qualifications to become a plumber. About a year ago he started his own plumbing business, employing one other guy. I get the impression that he doesn't particularly enjoy his job but he didn't say what he would prefer to do instead.

Although he seems quite guarded in revealing too much about his current personal situation, I came away feeling pleased that he divulged as much as he did about his early life. There was also a couple of moments when he appeared really emotional while recalling his childhood.

As I was leaving I asked if I could text him next week to meet up again but his reply was non-committal.

Am I any nearer to reuniting the two brothers? It's too early to say.

CHAPTER EIGHT:
RYAN

I like Sienna. She is charming and kind, the right person to look after my brother, but why oh why did she have to contact me?

Until she appeared on my doorstep I had compartmentalised my feelings towards Kieran. Of course I thought about him a lot but that was usually accompanied by extreme remorse for cutting him out of my life at such an early age.

I surprised myself at revealing my innermost thoughts about my father but surely Kieran must think the same about me? Or does his autistic brain somehow block those thoughts?

Sienna's recollection of Kieran's life has made me feel guilty that I wasn't there for him. I'm ashamed to admit I know very little about autism. In all these years I haven't even bothered to look into the possible reasons why Kieran behaved the way he did. There must be a wealth of material on the internet about autism that would give me some guidance to my brother's behaviours but for some reason I've never looked into it.

There's no time like the present so I access Google and type in 'autistic sleeping patterns' and it comes back with page after page of data. It's quite overwhelming. It mentions that a lot of autistic people have ADHD (attention deficient hyperactivity disorder) and anxiety which results in disruptive sleep. Another factor is they have sensory sensitivities to light, sound or touch which contributes to having difficulty sleeping. There are a couple of articles on medicines which focus on how ADHD adults or children often are given stimulants which causes insomnia. It's a minefield. As we're going off to sleep we produce Melatonin which is a natural hormone. Another report suggests that autistic people do not produce enough Melatonin and often have to be given it in tablet form. I do remember Mum giving Kieran a tablet just before he went to bed – I wonder if it was Melatonin? If so it didn't work.

I then type in 'typical autistic behaviours' and again it comes back with a lot of information. I'm trying to decipher what is relevant to Kieran from the following: 'Finding it hard to understand what others are thinking or feeling; getting very anxious about social situations; finding it difficult to make friends or preferring to be alone; having the same routine every day and getting very anxious if it changes.' From what I can remember all of these were applicable.

I'm curious to see what information there is on the aggressive side of autism and find a number of articles on this subject. One such piece was extremely interesting:

'Aggressive behaviours in children with autism often cause families a great deal of difficulty. Hitting, kicking, biting, throwing objects and other such reactions during a temper tantrum or meltdown can greatly increase parents' stress. These types of aggression may cause a child to be banned from community activities such as school programs, scouting or sports. Furthermore the fear of aggressive incidents may keep families at home, increasing their sense of isolation and decreasing their quality of life.'

I can relate to all of this. Whenever we went to the shops Kieran would always approach someone and usually stamp on their feet, flick their ears or lick their hands. I remember Mum getting really stressed out and having arguments with members of the public when trying to defend him. Although she would always let him know that he shouldn't be approaching people in that manner, she never shouted at him or got angry. At the time that really pissed me off. I mean why the fuck would he lick someone else's hand? What the hell was that all about? However, thinking about it now, Mum knew that Kieran couldn't help it so she was extremely tolerant, kind and patient with him.

That kindness was never extended to me.

I would often ask Mum why we didn't go out more often. I wanted to go to the shops or to the park or watch a film in the cinema but she just told me that was too difficult which probably meant that it involved bringing Kieran out as well and she was often reluctant to do that. Of course at the time I didn't understand any of that and it just made me more resentful towards her. I hated Kieran for stopping me doing the things I liked.

In recent years whenever there was a TV documentary about autism I immediately changed channels. I didn't want to be reminded of that dark period in my life.

But reading these articles has given me more of an understanding. I should be grateful that I wasn't born into autism and instead feel sorry for Kieran who drew the short straw.

Sienna suggested I should meet up with Mum but I'm not too keen on that. This is all moving too fast for me. I need time to think. Maybe I will have another meeting with Sienna. It felt comforting going through my past with her. She was very patient and tolerant with me even when I lost my rag. She's a great listener. There's no doubt her engaging personality made me divulge so much more than I intended to.

I type a text to her.

'Can you pop around on Monday? Same time?'

'Yes, I'll be there and I'll bring the wine.'

I smile at her reply which was a nice way to end a thought-provoking evening.

CHAPTER NINE:
SIENNA

I feel that I'm making progress with Ryan. Bit by bit he's opening up about his past but I've got to tread carefully because it could go either way.

I was delighted to receive his text last night agreeing to another meeting. If I could just get him to meet Sally I truly feel it will pave the way to reconciling with Kieran.

But it won't be easy. At the moment his bitterness seems more directed at his mother but I've yet to go into detail about his relationship with Kieran, so that could change. I tried to explain how difficult her life was, struggling to raise Kieran on her own and although he accepted some of the issues she faced, he's still so angry about the way he believes she treated him.

Sally has never talked in any great depth about her relationship with Ryan so I was somewhat surprised to hear how bad he felt he was treated by her. It'll be interesting to hear her version of events but I suspect there is an element of truth in what he told me.

This is yet another complicated family setup which is not going to be easy to resolve but I'm determined to see it through. If I do succeed, I might apply to the United Nations, for the world Peace Ambassador vacancy.

But today is the first performance in the Easter run of *Peter Pan*. As the Christmas pantomime season is so popular our local theatre also run an Easter pantomime. Although Easter is a few weeks away they put on a couple of performances to get the production ready, similarly to the work in progress performances that comedians do. I am taking Kieran, Jamie and Nicky. Mandy will also be there for extra support.

It's a professional production with actors from *Eastenders* and *Hollyoaks* but the entire audience is made up of special needs children and adults accompanied by their families and carers. A local charity has funded this special performance.

'Are you looking forward to seeing *Peter Pan*?' I ask Kieran as we approach the theatre.

'No.'

'Why's that?'

'I saw the *Peter Pan* cartoon film and it's just utter bullshit,' Kieran proclaims.

'Why?'

'Because he's flying all over the place. His feet never touch the pavement. I don't know anyone who flies, do you?'

'The story is fictional which means that it's made up. It's escapism from real life. I'm sure you'll enjoy it.'

'I won't. Can't we get a couple of KitKats instead?'

'Will the audience shout out 'he's behind you?' Jamie asks.

'Yes, that always happens in pantomime.'

'Well if they do they're going to get a bunch of fives from me.'

'Jamie, you won't get aggressive with any member of the audience, regardless of what they say. Do you understand?'

'Can I just spit at them instead?'

'No, there's going to be no punching or spitting. If you do that we'll be thrown out of the theatre.'

'Perfect, then I'll get back to see *Pointless*.'

And there I was thinking that a visit to the theatre was a joyous experience rather than an excuse for a punch up.

'Do all these people think that Pan character can fly? If they do they must be idiots,' Kieran remarks as he's looking at the audience. 'They certainly look like idiots, every one of them.'

'Kieran, I think we've exhausted the flying scenario, OK?'

'But Pan can't fly.'

I pretend I don't hear this last remark because when Kieran gets a bee in his bonnet about something it usually lasts a few hours.

Nicky is tapping everyone on the shoulder in the auditorium but it mostly gets a positive reaction. We're all in the same boat.

We take our seats which are in the second row. Maybe because we're so close to the action it will have a positive effect on our trio, or then again maybe not.

When the actors walk on stage for the first scene the joyous reaction from the audience is deafening. However, Nicky clasps his hands over his ears and rocks from side to side while Jamie shouts 'fuck off' to anyone within earshot but luckily the noise from the audience drowns him out.

This doesn't bode well.

A couple of minutes later Nicky takes off both his trainers and throws them onto the stage. This halts the scene as one of the actors picks them up and hands them back to Mandy, who holds onto them for dear life. Some of the audience laugh at Nicky's endeavours whilst those around us just stare at him with confused expressions.

There's a relatively quiet moment in the performance when Kieran shouts to the actors – 'you're all a bunch of bastards'. The actors actually stop to find out who gave them such a constructive critique. But Kieran's not finished yet. He stands up and points at Peter Pan and shouts 'you're a goddamn fraud cos you can't fly'.

Again all the cast look totally baffled. I manage to get Kieran to sit down and it isn't long before a security guard comes over to us.

''Look I know your guys are autistic but we simply can't have any more disruptions to the performance. It's not fair to the actors or the audience. Is that clear?' He asks me.

'Yes, my apologies.'

He nods and moves to the side of the stage, close enough to monitor the other performers of the afternoon (i.e. Kieran, Jamie and Nicky).

However it's only a few minutes later when the part of the show that I've been dreading is about to happen. One of the actors creeps up behind another performer and all the audience (with the exception of the fab three) shout 'he's behind you'.

Jamie stands up, turns around to face the audience and shouts 'have a shit and fuck off.'

I think that's our cue to leave.

As we exit the row some people start booing us, however the boy at the end of the row is laughing and clapping. He's the exception.

The security guard escorts us as we run the gauntlet to the back of the theatre and to the safety of the auditorium.

'I'm really sorry about that,' I explain to the guard.

'No need to apologise, I understand. There's a lot going on and it must be distressing for them.'

'Do you have any connection to autism?' I ask.

'No, but over the years I've been here for these special performances and I've seen similar reactions a number of times. I'm just sorry it didn't work out for you.'

'I like your suit, do you want it?' Jamie asks the guard.

'Yes, I think I'll keep it,' he replies with a smile.

'I'll give you a fiver for it.'

'OK, Jamie, I think it's time we left and let the security man get on with his job.'

'It was nice to meet you,' the guard says as we head towards the exit.

'OK, six pounds and thirty-five pence but that's my final offer,' Jamie shouts.

I guide Jamie out of the theatre before the guard has a chance to reply.

'Well that could've gone better,' Mandy says.

'Jamie, why did you have to shout obscenities at the audience?' I ask.

'They were being too silly and loud.'

'That's what happens in a pantomime.'

'Well I'll have nothing to do with it.'

And neither will we now.

'As we've got time on our hands what do we do now?' Mandy asks.

'Is Bob Denny playing anywhere near here?' Kieran asks. 'He's always doing shows in London.'

Bob Denny is a well known comedian.

'I don't think so but I'll google it,' I reply.

Kieran is a massive Bob Denny fan. Last year we went to see Bob Denny and that's just about the happiest

I've ever seen him. We were in the front row and during the act Bob picked Kieran for a duet to the Tom Jones song *Kiss*. Kieran was beside himself. There isn't a day that goes past when we doesn't play that video of him and Bob. I was so pleased I had the presence of mind to record it. He wrote to Bob afterwards and got a lovely letter and signed photo in return. He framed it and is now hanging up on his bedroom wall. It was a wonderful evening.

My only regret was that we didn't go to the stage door afterwards to get a photo. Well actually we did but Kieran insisted on having an ice cream straight after the performance and by the time we got there Bob was gone.

'Good news, Kieran. Bob Denny's going to play Wimbledon theatre next Tuesday. Do you want to go?'

'Are you kidding me? It's going to be the happiest day of my life.'

Now the pressure is on to get the tickets but somehow I don't think it's going to be a sell out. His popularity peaked in the mid-eighties. He's rarely on TV these days.

'The last time he told seventy-eight jokes. Sixty-five of them were funny but the other thirteen were shit. If he tells those shitty jokes again I'll boo him,' Kieran tells me.

Which is exactly what Kieran did the last time. It did get some strange looks from the people around us but as soon as they noticed the magical 'I have AUTISM please be patient' badge I think they understood.

'If you don't like the jokes just stay silent. He's doing his best and it's rude if you boo him.'

'But he needs to know that the jokes are crap so he doesn't tell them to anyone else for the rest of his life.'

When Kieran first started booing him Bob did glance down at us and I could tell he was about to launch into one of his well-rehearsed retorts until he too noticed the badge. I then thought that it was a sweet gesture on his behalf when he invited Kieran up on stage. He seems like a top guy and this time around I will make sure that Kieran has all the ice cream he needs before the end of the performance so we can head straight to the stage door.

As Jamie also likes comedians it has crossed my mind to also invite him to the Wimbledon gig but dealing with Kieran is stressful enough. And I think it's the right decision given Jamie's impromptu pantomime performance, however I will find another comedy event for him.

'Can we leave Leicester Square now?' Kieran asks me.

'Why? There's lots we can do here – we can go to the cinema or a meal or even to the pub?'

'There's too many people walking around so there's no room on the pavements.'

'What do you want to do instead?'

'Buy a packet of cheese and onion crisps in Finsbury Park.'

Sounds like an exciting night out.

'Can we just walk back to Finsbury Park? It's only 4.5 miles,' Jamie asks.

'But that'll take at least an hour and a half,' Mandy pleads.

'But we left that silly play after only seventeen minutes and it lasts for two hours and five minutes so we've saved one hour and forty-eight minutes. If we walk now we'll arrive back thirty-five minutes earlier than even staying to the end of the play and taking the tube back. I like thirty-five minutes extra sleep, don't you?'

How can I argue with that logic?

So we walk the 4.5 miles back to the home. At least this should make them all tired and hopefully they'll be able to get a good night's sleep.

Nicky must have touched about fifty people along the way. I started counting but stopped at thirty-three. The reason why I do this is when we meet up with the medical professionals to review his medication I like to provide them with actual facts concerning his OCD behaviour. He stamped his foot on four members of the public, two of which were really pissed off even after I explained everything.

After having dinner back at the house everyone settled into their bedrooms with minimum fuss. Jamie's suggestion in walking back was a good one.

I arrive back at my flat in Pimlico and grab a bottle of wine from the fridge. It was always going to be a risk taking three autistic adults to the theatre but I really expected our visit to last longer than seventeen minutes. Those seventeen minutes were somewhat eventful – Nicky throwing his trainers onto the stage, Kieran calling the actors a bunch of bastards and telling Peter Pan that he was a goddamn fraud. But the icing on the cake was Jamie telling the audience to have a shit and fuck off.

All in a day's work.

CHAPTER TEN:
RYAN

In a few minutes Sienna will be coming around again but this time I'm looking forward to her visit. She's a genuinely nice person who has only got Kieran's best interests at heart. She's going above and beyond her job description to try and reconcile me with my brother.

Before her last visit I was reluctant to discuss my past with her. All I wanted out of that meeting was to find out what's been happening with Kieran but she kept probing me about my relationship with him and Mum and I must admit it felt good to verbalise some of my feelings that I've kept to myself for too many years.

But her suggestion about meeting with Mum threw me. I suppose from her point of view it made sense as she picked up on the bitterness I still feel towards my mother and before I could even think about seeing Kieran my issues with my mother needed to be resolved first.

But am I ready to see my mother again? I don't think so but I am curious to know if she's apologetic for the way she treated me back then or will she just justify her actions by hiding behind Kieran's many issues? I have no idea.

But my thoughts are interrupted by the sound of the doorbell. It's therapy time.

'How are you keeping?' Sienna asks as I let her in.

'Yeah, not bad I suppose.'

She hands me a cold bottle of Chardonnay.

'You shouldn't have,' I say.

'Let's take it in turns. You're next.'

'Will there be a next time?'

'I certainly hope so.'

Sienna ticks all the boxes. She's attractive, kind, compassionate and with a lovely sense of humour. I know very little about her personal life. She doesn't wear a ring but does that mean anything these days? In different circumstances I might even ask her out for a date but then again I'm hardly a catch. When I left home I had a number of one night stands. The first few times this happened was exciting for me but the novelty wore off pretty quickly. From that point to the present day the longest I've been in a relationship has been nine months and it's nearly always been me who ends it. Have my issues with my mother installed a mistrust of all women? The last relationship I was in lasted nearly six months. The pattern is usually the same, the first two to three months are just great. Everything is new, neither of us showing the negative side of our personalities but as time moves on and the first arguments occur I lose patience very quickly. I just can't bear the thought of going back to a fractured relationship; too many bad memories. So maybe it is all pointing back to my mother.

I hand Sienna a glass of wine.

'Cheers,' I say.

'Cheers.'

We click glasses.

'So what are we talking about today?' I ask.

'Can we discuss the issues with your mother?'

'I thought we already had.'

'I got the feeling we only scratched the surface.'

'Well I told you that she completely ignored me throughout most of my childhood because all her efforts were directed at Kieran. He couldn't put a foot wrong whereas I couldn't do anything right. So I grew up resenting her and Kieran and that's the reason why I left. It's as simple as that.'

'But do you really want to go through the rest of your life hating your mother for mistakes that she made? That can't be good? Don't you want to hear her side of the story?'

'But it won't change anything, will it?'

'Perhaps not but don't you think it's time you made amends before it's too late?'

'Why? She's not ill, is she?'

'No, she isn't but you never know what's going to happen, do you?'

'I've done nothing wrong, but let me ask you how you get on with your mum?'

'This isn't about me.'

'I know, but you've asked me some really personal questions that are totally outside of your remit, which is primarily caring for my brother. I'm just curious what your relationship is like with your mother. You don't have to answer it if you don't want to.'

'Is this just a diversionary tactic?'

'No, but don't you think it'll make me more co-operative if you reveal a bit more about your life? That's only fair.'

'So it's emotional blackmail then?' She replies, smiling.

'That's a rather harsh way of putting it but if you're not willing to talk about your mother then perhaps we can discuss another topic? The weather? The political situation in Peru...'

'OK, you've made your point. As a matter of fact my situation is the reverse of yours. My mother had an affair and when my father found out he immediately wanted a divorce.'

'So what happened?'

'Apparently the affair had been going on for just over a year. He was a work colleague. When this all came to light my mother moved in with this guy and I stayed with my father.'

'Wow, how old were you?'

'Twelve.'

'Have you got any brothers or sisters?'

'No.'

'So are you still in contact with your mother?'

'Yes, I never really had any issues with her. She just made a big mistake and paid the price.'

'Didn't things work out with the guy?'

'No, he was only interested in the physical side of their relationship. She only stayed with him for a few weeks before they split. Dad got her a rented flat nearby and when the divorce went through she was able to purchase a small house.'

'Did she ever want to come back?'

'Yes, but Dad told her the trust was gone and that was that.'

'Did he ever find someone else?'

'No. He wasn't interested. He's a good guy and felt very let down. He was and still is an amazing father.'

'So we're both from broken homes, although our circumstances are very different. You seem much more adjusted to it.'

'I didn't have an autistic brother to contend with.'

'But knowing you, I'm sure you would've dealt with it a lot better than I did.'

'Can we talk about your mother now?'

'What else do you want to know?'

'There must've been some good times with her?'

'Maybe there was but it could only have been before Kieran came along and I was too young to remember that period.'

'But she can't have treated you badly the whole time after your brother's issues began to unravel?'

'Why don't you ask her that question?'

'Why don't you? I'm know that she's desperate to see you again.'

I take a large gulp of wine. Sienna will not leave me be until I agree with her request. I've avoided this situation for way too long so is it time to face up to my past and confront my mother over all these issues that I've buried within me for so long?

To quote Elvis, 'it's now or never'.

'OK, let's do it,' I proclaim.

'Wow, what made you change your mind?'

'You convinced me that as my mother won't be around forever I need to clear the air with her once and for all. It's something that I've been putting off for years. I'm not hopeful that she'll give me any sort of explanation that will justify her actions but if she's willing to meet up then I'll be there. Rest assured I won't back out.'

'I think you've made the right decision.'

'I'm not sure about that but only time will tell. Now that you've got what you came for can you relax a bit and have a bite to eat? I've just made some lasagne.'

'Sounds great. Anyway I thought I was relaxed?'

'You're like a dog with a bone but I'm OK with that. You have good intentions. More wine?'

'Yes please. So can I ask you a personal question?' She asks.

'You've been asking me nothing but so far.'

'It's really personal.'

'Go ahead.'

'Has your issues with your mother affected your relationships with women?'

'You're not backwards in coming forward are you? I was actually thinking along the same lines when you arrived here today. Although I'm not really into all that psychological claptrap I hear so often from all those precious celebrities, I'm beginning to think that I do mistrust women and it's possibly linked to my painful relationship with my mother. I'm assuming you're thinking along the same lines?'

'I did wonder but I'm sorry, it's really none of my business.'

'No, don't apologise. To my surprise I'm actually enjoying talking about my past. If I went to a professional consultant it'll cost me a lot and you're free.'

'And I brought a bottle of wine.'

'Yes you did and a glass or two of that would be more than enough for me to divulge all my secrets.'

'Seriously though, I'm so pleased that you've agreed to meet your mother.'

'So when will you contact her?'

'Tonight when I get home.'

'Because she now lives so far away I would imagine it'll take time to set up?'

'No, quite the contrary. I've got a feeling she'll get the first train out of Blackburn, so be prepared for that.'

I'm now beginning to feel nervous and slightly sick at the very real prospect of seeing the person who has caused me more anguish than anyone else in my life.

'Can you remember your thoughts when you first moved out of the family home?' She asks.

'Jeez, you're relentless,' I reply with a smile.

'I'm sorry, I didn't mean…'

'No, I'm only kidding. Yes, I can remember it all very clearly. It was like a massive weight had been lifted off my shoulders. That first night I thought I'd sleep like a log but I hardly slept at all. It was a strange feeling being on my own. I used to wake up several times in the night because of Kieran, even though I knew he wasn't in the house, but I just couldn't settle. I know that doesn't make much sense but that's the way it was and that insomnia continued for quite a while. Even now I don't sleep that great.'

'Do you think about Kieran when you're awake at night?'

'Yes, sometimes, but it's usually the normal things that everyone else worries about, money issues, relationships etc. At night these problems always seem much worse don't they?'

'Yes they do.'

'Anyway I think the lasagne is ready so let's eat.'

We spend the next hour just chin-wagging. I deliberating avoid any discussion about my family. Sienna did tell me that she's just out of a relationship but only mentioned this in passing. I'd love to find out more details.

She asked earlier whether I had had any female relationship issues. It's almost like she knew about my past after only a couple of meetings. She was very astute in linking that to all my issues with my mother; a very clever lady.

I lay in bed feeling anxious at the prospect of meeting my mother after fourteen years. Perhaps Sienna's suggestion of arranging a quick meeting is a good one because I won't get much sleep until that happens.

CHAPTER ELEVEN: SIENNA

'I've just met your son,' I tell Sally.

'Oh my God, how is he?'

'He's fine and he's agreed to see you.'

'I can't believe it. I've been trying for years to achieve what you've done in your first discussion with him. What the hell did you say?'

'First of all I have to confess it was our third meeting.'

'I don't understand, I thought I told you to let me know exactly what you were doing. I think my precise words were keep me informed every step along the way. That was our agreement.'

'I know and I'm sorry but let me explain. On our first meeting he didn't want to know. He only spoke to me for about a minute before shutting the door in my face. Maybe I should've told you then but I didn't want to hurt your feelings.'

'I would've expected that reaction from him.'

'I was going to give it a few days before contacting you just in case he changed his mind but the next day he texted me and wanted to meet up.'

'Do you know why?'

'No, he didn't say. I did put some recent photos of Kieran through the letter box so maybe that persuaded him.'

'So what did he have to say when you met again?'

'It took a bit of gentle probing but he was surprisingly candid about his past. He told me about some of the difficulties he faced growing up.'

'Please don't keep me in suspense…'

'Well it's probably no surprise to learn that he's very bitter towards you. He told me that you basically ignored him throughout most of his childhood as all your efforts were taken up with Kieran. He said that he was completely left to his own devices. He's still so angry about that.'

'So if he feels like that why has he agreed to see me?'

'He wants to hear what you have to say. You could explain to him all the intense pressures you were under at the time.'

'Do you believe that I was a bad parent to him?'

'My opinion doesn't matter. This is between you and Ryan. After talking to me at length we agreed that before he sees Kieran he needs to get some sort of reconciliation with you. Why don't you just tell me what happened?'

'So you want me to justify myself to you first before I see my son?'

'No, of course not. I just thought that it might be easier if you explained everything to me first then perhaps I can give you some advice on how to approach him. I've got some idea on what sets him off so this just has to be handled carefully. That's all.'

'My apologies if I'm coming off too aggressive, it's just this has come as a bit of a shock and my stomach's in knots right now.'

'No problem. He's going to ask you some really blunt questions and I think you need to be prepared for that.'

'You know, Ryan's right. I wasn't there for him when he was growing up. Kieran took up all my energy and thoughts, I just didn't have anything else to give and Ryan paid the price. I've lived with that regret since the day he left home. I'm not sure I can offer him any sort of explanation that will satisfy him because there isn't one but all I can do is apologise and hope and pray that he'll forgive me and maybe one day we can rebuild our relationship. However, I've very low expectations that that will ever happen. But you've given me an opportunity that I never thought I'd get so I've got to make the most of it and hope for the best.'

'I think you've just said it all. When do you want me to arrange this? Ryan seems flexible enough.'

'Tomorrow if possible. I've waited for this moment for over fourteen years and I don't want to wait any longer.'

'I think tomorrow will be OK. He also seems eager to get this done as quickly as possible. I'll ring Ryan now and let you know straight away.'

'One more thing. Can you be with us? You've always been amazing with Kieran. He's a different person now and that's all down to you. And now you've pulled off the impossible in contacting Ryan and somehow persuading him to see me. I still can't believe it. Please say you'll come?'

'I hadn't intended coming but if it's OK with Ryan then I'll be there.'

'Thank you for everything.'

'You're more than welcome, now let me ring Ryan.'

My conversation with Ryan barely lasts a minute. He agrees to meet up tomorrow evening at a pub in Kings Cross. I then contact Sally who does the same.

Both of the conversations were subdued, they obviously have a lot on their minds.

CHAPTER TWELVE: SIENNA

'Why doesn't that Johnson character sort out his goddam hair? Can't he afford a comb?' Kieran asks

'Are you talking about Boris Johnson?'

'Yeah, the fat one. His hair's all over the place. Shall we have a whip around to buy him a comb?'

'No, I don't think that's necessary. He just likes the unkempt look.'

'I comb my hair every hour and if I saw that idiot I'd comb his too. It worries me to see it flopping all over the place.'

I can confirm that Kieran does comb his hair very thoroughly every hour on the hour. It's just one of his many severe OCD behaviours.

'Boris Johnson has a lot of security around him so I don't think you'll be able to get anywhere near him.'

'That won't be a problem. I'll just kick those security guys in the balls. It's simple. Anyway I wrote him a letter.'

Kieran hands me a piece of paper. It reads as follows:

'Dear Johnson, Your hair is a disgrace. It makes me want to vomit. Why can't you comb it for fucks sake? Also you need to lose weight. What size waist are you?

I'm guessing it's forty-four inches. I don't like fat people. Anyway if you need any advice on your hair and getting rid of some of that fat just write to me and I'll put you straight. Yours faithfully, Kieran. PS That posh accent of yours is hideous, so just lose it. A Birmingham accent will suit you much better.'

I smile to myself as I read Kieran's latest letter. He loves writing to famous people and unless there are swear words involved I usually post them for him. It's surprising how many nice replies he gets despite the fact that some of the contents of his letters are, shall we say, rather blunt.

I'll post Kieran's letter to Boris Johnson this morning and await his reply.

'So what shall we do today?' I ask. I like to give him an option and if the answer is practical I try to make it happen.

'Can we go to Berlin?'

'Berlin, Germany?'

'Yeah, that's it.'

'And why do you want to go there?'

'I want to find out if the Germans speak with an Adolf Hitler accent?'

'How much do you know about Hitler?' I ask.

'He was always pissed off and had a small moustache.'

'Did you know that his political party killed millions of people during the Second World War?'

'Yeah, but maybe he was just in a bad mood during the war and couldn't get his hands on any tablets to calm him down?'

Six years is a long time to be in a bad mood.

'Kieran, he was a very evil man.'

'Maybe he should've had a few Guinnesses? That would've made him feel better.'

'Germans speak with a German accent, not an Adolf Hitler accent. I don't think even if Hitler had a couple of pints of Guinness every night that things would've been that much better during the Second World War but that's an interesting theory. I'm afraid Berlin is too far to visit today, sorry. Is there anything else you want to do?'

'Will I see my mum again before I get any grey hairs?'

That remark may sound a little sarcastic but Kieran really doesn't do sarcasm.

'Of course you will. I'll speak to her today and arrange a date and time for her visit.'

I don't want to tell him that Sally is probably already on a London-bound train as I'm not sure she'll be in the right frame of mind to see Kieran after meeting up with Ryan.

'I remember my father was very tall and had blue eyes. He also liked wearing white t-shirts but only the ones that had a collar. Is he dead now?'

'As far as I know he's still alive but it's best to speak to your mother about that.'

'I think I was twelve when he left home. I thought he was going to the pub that night so I waited for him to come back as he always brought me a packet of cheese and onion crisps from the pub. Mum kept telling me to go to bed but I waited for hours for my crisps and then fell asleep on the sofa. Mum bought me three packets of cheese and onion crisps the next day so that made me feel better.'

I smile but I'm too choked up to respond. This is the first time that he's mentioned his father to me. It's almost as if he's aware of a forthcoming family reunion. But he can't know that, surely?

Sally and Ryan portray Kieran's father as a cold and cruel man and it seems his only redeeming quality was the fact that he regularly forked out for a packet of cheese and onion crisps for Kieran.

'Did he leave because I farted too much?'

'No, I'm pretty sure that wasn't the reason but again speak to your mother about that.'

I'm already in over my head with this family so I'll let Sally field any father questions from Kieran.

'I only slept for seventy-three minutes last night,' Kieran tells me, the master of changing the subject. Any discussion away from his father is a relief right now.

'Yes, I know. The night staff informed me. Why couldn't you sleep?'

'It's all Bob Denny's fault.'

'Is it because you're excited about seeing him tomorrow night?'

'Yes and in my seventy-three minutes of sleep I dreamt about Bob.'

'And what was your dream about?'

'Bob and me arrived at the theatre on horses and I did the opening song with him.'

'And what was the song?'

'*Walking In The Air.*'

I'd pay top dollar to see that combo.

'Well you won't have to wait long before you can see him again.'

'Thirty-three hours and seventeen minutes,' Kieran replies after a quick glance at the clock on the wall.

'So any ideas on what you want to do today?' I ask again.

'Can we walk to Finsbury Park and look at the grass?'

'Yeah sure, no problem.'

All the carers at StarLight are fully trained to accompany the residents when outside the boundaries of the care home but we have to be one hundred percent focused at all times. For example taking Nicky out for a walk is somewhat precarious as he shows no sense of danger on road safety. If he sees a sweet shop on the other side of the street he would just blindly walk onto the road without taking any notice of the traffic. I've never seen Nicky look at the oncoming cars, so consequently we have to hold his hand tightly when crossing the road. The problem with Kieran is different. Although he's aware of road safety he is extremely impatient at waiting, which usually means when the first gap in traffic appears he dashes across the road even if cars are heading towards him at speed. It can be quite frightening and on a number of occasions cars have come to a screeching halt when he goes on one of his suicide missions. He's been lectured on road safety many times but his ADHD seems to conquer any such safety thoughts.

From time to time Kieran mentions that he wants to drive. I'm not sure what the law is about autistic adults driving but he would make James Bond look like an eighty-eight-year-old man driving at ten miles an hour. He's always telling me to go through the red light if he's in a hurry or just crash through the cars if we're in a traffic jam. Even when I try to explain how dangerous this is he just says 'it's not a big deal, just do it.'

However, today the traffic is slow and we reach Finsbury Park without getting run over.

'I like grass, it makes me smile,' Kieran informs me. 'What country invented it?'

'It wasn't really invented, it's just part of nature.'

'I don't like it when it's raining as there's too much mud and it sticks to my trainers so I always have to put them in the washing machine. I only like grass when it's dry.'

Kieran is quiet as we walk through the park; he's busy taking in his grass surroundings. I decide to ask him something that's been bothering me since the first day I met him.

'Why did you spit at me?'

'You smiled too much.'

'And why did that bother you?'

'It pissed me off that you were so happy.'

'Were you unhappy then?'

'I'm not happy very often.'

'That makes me sad to hear you say that.'

'Singing with Bob Denny made me happy though.'

'But you don't mind me smiling now so what changed?'

'You used to always have tissue wipes with you and whenever I spat at you you wiped the spit off straight away but one day when we were shopping you didn't have the wipes so you had to clean it with your shirt sleeve but that didn't work properly, so you now had two stains on your shirt the whole time we were shopping. I didn't like that so I stopped spitting at you just in case you didn't have a wipe. I didn't want to take that risk.'

Did I really expect a straight forward reply?

'What else makes you happy?'

'I like seeing trees with no leaves on them.'

'So you must be happy during winter?'

'No, because I have to wear a jumper and a jacket and they weigh too much.'

'OK, does anything else make you feel good?'

After about two minutes of contemplation he shakes his head.

So Kieran's happiness depends on Bob Denny, trees with no leaves and grass. Not all obvious choices but each to their own.

'Shall we go back to your home now?' I ask.

'Can I just look at few more blades of grass first?'

'OK, no problem.'

I really enjoyed our walk in the dry grass. We had a nice chat but it was distressing to hear Kieran mention that most of the time he's unhappy. Although this doesn't come as a shock to me it's still sad to hear him verbalise it. However this will only make me more determined than ever to orchestrate his reunion with Ryan.

I arrive at the pub fifteen minutes early. I notice Sally straight away. She's sitting in the far corner of the pub, almost as if she doesn't want to be seen.

'Can I get you another drink?' I ask as I approach her table.

'Yes please.'

'Is that whisky?' I ask.

She nods. I get our drinks and return to the table.

'You look nervous,' I say, stating the bleeding obvious.

'I am and have been since our last telephone conversation. I just can't foresee any positive outcome. There's nothing I can say that justifies what I did or more to the point what I didn't do.'

'I appreciate that this is so difficult for you but please have faith. The fact that he's willing to see you must give you some hope?'

'I just think that ultimately it's going to be the final nail in the coffin. Although I always held little hope of ever seeing Ryan again there was still the slightest chance that somehow time would heal our differences but now that day has arrived I fear that by the end of this evening I will never see him again.'

'Remember what we talked about on the phone? Just be honest with him and try to explain what you were going through at that time. Not only were you dealing with all of Kieran's problems but you were also trying to cope with your husband's infidelity and his total lack of support, whether financial or emotional, for you and your sons. You've got to believe that somehow Ryan will realise that you were under intense pressure and that there were mitigating circumstances.'

Sally is staring at the pub entrance and standing there is Ryan.

CHAPTER THIRTEEN:
SIENNA

'Let me have a quick chat with him first,' I tell Sally.

She takes a sip of her whisky and simply nods.

'We're in the corner,' I say to Ryan, pointing towards his mother. 'let me get you a drink, what are you having?'

'A pint of lager please.'

He glances at Sally but there's no acknowledgement.

As expected this is going to be tough.

'So how are you feeling?' I ask.

'Nervous as hell.'

'Well your mother feels the same way.'

He's tapping his fingers on the bar as he waits for his drink.

'Ryan, all I ask is that you give her a chance to talk to you otherwise this will all be a waste of time.'

'That's what I'm here for,' he replies. He's edgy but I suppose that's understandable.

'Let's do it,' he adds as he picks up his glass.

Sally stands up as Ryan approaches her table. She holds her arms towards him in the hope of an embrace but he ignores the gesture and sits down opposite her. She looks crestfallen.

'How are you?' Sally asks her son after an awkward silence.

'That's probably the first time you've ever asked about my welfare. Correct me if I'm wrong?'

'You're not wrong.'

More silence follows. Despite my intention to take a backseat I feel I need to intervene.

'Sally, why don't you give Ryan an update on Kieran?'

'We all multi task every single day, don't we?' Ryan asks his mother, ignoring my question to her.

'Yes, I suppose so,' she replies.

'Of course I realise that you were dealing with an autistic child and all the problems that that entailed but did it ever occur to you that you completely neglected me every single day? Did that thought ever cross your mind?'

'Yes, it did but I just couldn't cope.'

'You didn't attend any of the parents-teachers meetings, you never went along to any of the school plays that I was in, you never once helped me with my homework, I could be here all night listing all the things that you didn't do but worse than any of this is that you never showed me any love. All your love was directed at Kieran. I remember you shouting at me because I didn't finish my dinner, yet Kieran regularly threw his dinner on the floor and I don't remember you ever raising your voice at him. We've never had a civil discussion and this all has affected me right up to today so I hope that you're happy about inflicting such psychological damage to me for so many years.'

'Ryan, I'm just so sorry...'

'Is that it then? A mumbled apology is enough? Soon after I left home I saw a psychiatrist but he pissed me off as he kept giving me feeble explanations on why you acted the way you did. I wasn't having it so I packed that in quickly enough. I was so angry, in fact this is all a fucking waste of time. I don't know why I even agreed to this, I'm leaving.'

Ryan gets up and starts to walk away.

'When you were asleep I often kissed you,' Sally tells her son.

'You're lying,' Ryan angrily replies.

'No, I'm not.'

'So why didn't you do that when I was awake?'

'Occasionally I did. I should've done it more but I was just so stressed out with Kieran. I couldn't think straight.'

'I don't remember you ever kissing me.'

'It was when you were very young. Maybe you've subconsciously blocked out those few tender moments. I always felt on the verge of a nervous breakdown. Kieran wouldn't sleep and I was always up with him. I went to the doctor and he prescribed some anti-depressant drugs and sleeping tablets but I couldn't take the sleeping tablets as I needed to be with Kieran throughout the night. A number of times he opened the front door to go for walks on his own. Of course I always caught up with him but on a few occasions he nearly got knocked over when crossing the road. If I hadn't been with him I'm not sure what would've happened because he has no sense of danger and would think nothing of walking out into a busy road without even looking. That thought kept me up most nights even when he was asleep as my fear was always that he would get out without me and that would not end well. I even locked the front door but he just smashed the living room window and got out that way.'

Ryan returns to our table and sits down.

'There were a few nights when I thought about ending it all. I just couldn't see a way out of my nightmare.'

Sally starts crying so I put my arm around her and stroke her hair. Ryan looks shocked at her confession but doesn't attempt to comfort his mother.

'I've never spoken to anyone about that but let me reassure you, Ryan, that what I've just told you is the absolute truth.'

'I believe you,' Ryan replies.

'As you're well aware Kieran was extremely aggressive and within twelve months of you leaving he broke my arm twice. The first time happened when I just asked him to eat his broccoli and he just went berserk. Your father was no longer around so it was just me and Kieran in the house. I always felt very vulnerable. The second time was when I tried to stop him from licking a stranger's face. He's less violent now and much of that is due to the amazing work that Sienna has done. She's the only person who has not been fazed with whatever Kieran does and she's basically turned his life around, for the better I might add. I owe her everything.'

Ryan glances at me and simply nods his head.

'I'll perfectly understand if this is the last time we see each other but please give your brother another chance. He's changed and he needs you.'

Ryan stares at the floor. The harsh account of the physical attacks on Sally plus her suicide confession has halted his tirade against his mother but he remains silent.

'Ryan, I'm going to leave now. I just want you to know that I'm deeply sorry for the way I treated you for so many years. Whatever Kieran's problems were

I should never have taken my anger and frustration out on you. I'll regret that for the rest of my life. Please try and find it in your heart to forgive me. I cannot tell you how unbelievable it is to see you again. I'll leave it up to you if you want to contact me again, Sienna has my details.'

Sally gets up and kisses the top of Ryan's head before walking away.

'Do you want another whisky?' Ryan asks his mother.

She turns around and nods.

'We have a lot to discuss, please sit down,' Ryan says.

Sally starts to cry but this time Ryan gets up, puts his arms around her and strokes her back. She rests her head on his shoulder. They stay in that position for nearly five minutes without speaking.

Sally isn't the only person in the pub shedding tears, she's joined by another two.

CHAPTER FOURTEEN: RYAN

'As I've got older I can see more clearly how much strain you were under dealing with Kieran and of course my so called father, but what I can't get my head around is why you didn't seem to devote any time to me at all? You seemed to resent me for not being autistic,' I say to my mother.

'Maybe subconsciously I felt bitter that Kieran was dealt such a cruel hand in life when you got off scot-free? But the truth is I was just so physically and mentally exhausted every single day that I didn't have the energy to give you any love and attention. My total focus was on Kieran and I know that was so wrong.'

'But didn't you ever feel guilty?'

'Yes I did but that was usually when I was lying in bed at night waiting for Kieran to go on his walkabouts.'

'But it obviously didn't make you do anything about it?'

'As I said earlier I did go into your bedroom to kiss you and apologise.'

'But what good was that when I was asleep?' Although I'm still feeling anger I'm not raising my voice and trying to tone down the aggression.

'I know, I know…'

Another moment of uncomfortable silence breaks the conversation.

'And of course your father was no help whatsoever. I can only remember a couple of occasions when he got up at night to help Kieran.'

'Have you heard anything from the bastard?' I ask my mother.

'No but I did receive a Christmas card from him, although it was not in his handwriting so I'm assuming his partner wrote it.'

'Wow, that's rubbing salt in the wound.'

'Maybe his partner feels some sympathy for me? Who knows? But I did take great pleasure in taking a match to it.'

'That's a real shame he's still alive. Did you get anything out of the divorce?'

'Eventually, but he was determined to give me next to nothing. However I was really lucky in hiring an excellent lawyer.'

'Well that's good news at least. What did you ever see in him? I don't get it. He has no redeeming qualities whatsoever.'

'I never did tell you how we met. We were in the same class at school. He was a bit of a Jack the lad, always joking and paying zero attention to his school work. Normally I'd run a mile from such a person but he started chatting me up and I suppose I was flattered. We dated for about a year before he proposed.'

'And how did he do that? I dread to think.'

'We were in a Wimpy bar and just as he bit into his burger and with a full mouthful he just said 'we might as well get married'. It was as simple as that.'

'And they said that romance is dead. Why the hell did you say yes? Surely you must've seen the writing on the wall?'

'It all looks much clearer in hindsight. I made a big mistake and boy did I pay the price. As the big day approached I was having serious doubts and wanted to call it off but Mum and Dad convinced me that it was just wedding nerves. They would've lost a lot of money if it didn't go ahead and that was also on my mind.'

'Did you know all about his affairs?'

'Not before we were married but soon after.'

'Did you confront him?'

'Yes, at first he denied it and actually got really angry that I had the nerve to accuse him but as time went on he did admit to his infidelities. I should've left him after his first admission but there was just too much going with Kieran to properly deal with my marriage issues. It got to the stage where he would tell me in great detail what he got up to in the bedroom with his female acquaintances. He was a cruel man.'

'Sienna tells me that you're living in Blackburn with a guy. Who is he?' I ask.

'His name's Robert. He's the lawyer that helped secure my future with the divorce. He's a decent, kind man. We're very happy together.'

'But why move to Blackburn?'

'That's where Robert's originally from. His elderly parents still live there and he wanted to be near them. We've got a nice house in a lovely area. I think we'll settle there. My only worry is being so far away from Kieran but Robert has assured me that he will drive me down here whenever I want. He understands my situation.'

'Has he met Kieran?'

'No, but that's down to me. I don't want to confuse or upset Kieran just now, it has to be handled very carefully but they will meet up soon enough. Speaking of which have you decided if you're going to see your brother?'

'No, not yet.'

Meeting my mother is traumatic enough. I need time to think about the next step.

'Did Kieran ever mention me after I left?' I ask.

'About a week after you'd gone he asked where you disappeared to so I just told him you've moved to another house.'

'And what did he say to that?'

'He told me he missed head-butting you and pinching your arm.'

I smile at my mother for the first time since we've met up.

'How do you think he'd handle it if I see him again? Be honest.'

'My fear is that he might regress to his aggressive behaviours as soon as he sees you. After all you were his punch bag. But I really do think it's a risk worth taking as ultimately he'd just love to see you again.'

'I really don't know what to do for the best.'

'Please don't put too much pressure on yourself. Just take your time to think about what's best for everybody.'

'I just can't believe that you're here right now and we're not shouting at each other. It seems like a miracle to me,' I say.

'Me too. I've waited fourteen years for this day and I've got Sienna to thank for this. She's a remarkable woman.'

'Yes she is. She's pulled off the impossible, not only in getting us back together but also transforming the life of my brother. We have to do something for her.'

'I totally agree but right now I think I'll make my way back to the hotel. It's been a long, tiring day. I can't tell you how thrilled I am to see you again.'

My mother gets up and gives me a hug. It feels good, if a little strange. I can't remember ever receiving hugs off her before today but maybe there were as I've seemingly blocked out the memory of her ever kissing me. I arrange for an Uber to take her back to the hotel. I then return to the pub to reflect on an unforgettable evening.

Soon after Sienna realised that I had calmed down and was having an amicable conversation with my mother she left us to it. She told us that this was a private matter between mother and son.

The way this evening has panned out has been a total surprise to me. I went in with all guns blazing, offloading all the anger and anxiety that I've kept inside me for way too long. She looked frightened and apologised a number of times but that didn't curtail my rage. I don't ever remember feeling so incensed as I did in those first few minutes of meeting my mother. So what changed? Her comment about kissing me when I was asleep threw me but what really stopped me in my tracks was when she revealed that on several occasions she contemplated suicide. For the first time I began to see everything from her perspective. When she told me that Kieran had broken her arm twice, I couldn't help but feel sorry for her situation at that time. Her husband left her to it after the humiliation of several affairs and soon after I moved out. She then had to deal with an autistic teenager on her own, whom she had raised virtually single-handedly since the day Kieran came into this world.

However the bitterness that I feel towards her has not disappeared after just one evening; that will take much longer.

So where do I go from here? My intention is to keep in contact with my mother and hopefully one day I will meet Robert. I am genuinely happy that she has finally found a loving relationship. Robert helped my mother out in her hour of need.

But what about Kieran? My mother's comment about her concerns that he may revert to his aggressive ways on meeting me again is on my mind. I don't know what to do for the best but I know one person who will.

CHAPTER FIFTEEN:
SIENNA

'I'd like to just hang out with Kieran at the home, if that's OK?.' Sally texted me last night.

Normally Sally takes Kieran out to the shops or to a restaurant but I know only too well that can be extremely stressful so she decided to see how it would be spending time with him in his most comfortable environment. Remarkably, she's never done that before.

Sally arrives early as she's travelling back to Blackburn this afternoon. In her text she asked if we could have a quick chat before seeing Kieran so whilst he is in his bedroom watching TV we meet up in the dining room.

'How did you think it went yesterday?' Sally nervously asks me.

'Unbelievably well. It was a tricky start but I suppose that's to be expected. I can't tell how pleased I was to see you both reconnecting with each other again after the initial outbursts. I hope that continued after I left?'

'Yes it did. I don't think I've completely won him over but it went so much better than I anticipated. To be able to have some sort of a relationship with Ryan is something I never thought would happen again and when he started to walk out of the pub after only a few minutes I really thought that would be the last I'd ever see him.'

'But he came back after you told him that you used to kiss him when he was asleep. He obviously didn't expect to hear that.'

'Yeah, something as simple as that changed the whole tone of our discussion. I just wished I'd shown more affection when he was awake. All the accusations that he made against me were true and I just feel ashamed that I've messed up a part of his life.'

'You can't change that now but he seemed to take on board your circumstances at the time so the important thing now is to rebuild your relationship with him and make up for lost time. It looks like he's willing to take that next step.'

'I hope so. I did ask him about seeing his brother but he was non-committal.'

'Funny you should say that because literally a few minutes before you arrived he texted me to ask if we can meet up again, so I'm assuming he wants to chat about Kieran.'

'If anyone can persuade him to meet Kieran it's you.'

'No pressure then,' I reply, smiling.

A few minutes later Kieran walks into the dining room. He approaches Sally and promptly spits on her face. She always has tissue wipes in her handbag so she wipes away the spittle without reprimanding her son. It's another one of Kieran's OCD behaviours that his mother has been on the receiving end on for as long as I've known him.

'And how are you today?' Sally asks Kieran.

'Are we going to Sainsbury's?'

'No, I'm staying here for a change. Shall we go for a stroll around the gardens?'

'That's a crap thing to do. It's for shitty people. I need to go to Sainsbury's.'

'Why?'

'I like their orange sign and I just love their KitKats.'

I'm not entirely certain what makes Sainsbury's KitKats so unique but I'm sure if I ask Kieran that question he will give me an extremely detailed explanation.

'Can I see your bedroom? It's been a while since I was up there.'

'It just has a bed and wallpaper. It also has a window but that's no use now as it's always locked.'

When I first arrived here there were a couple of incidents when Kieran climbed out of his bedroom window and landed on the roof of the dining room below it. This is only about a three foot drop but then he would jump from there into the garden which is about nine feet further down. The second time he did this he injured his right ankle so the window was then permanently locked, putting an end to his Spiderman impersonation.

'OK, you don't want me to see your bedroom so what else shall we do?'

'If you'd come earlier we could've watched Naga Munchetty on BBC Breakfast.'

'I didn't know you were interested in the news?'

'I'm not. The news is wasting my time. I just like looking at Munchetty's hair. She always keeps it short so it never gets out of hand.'

Kieran does have a thing about hair as Boris Johnson will soon find out.

'I need another thirty-one combs for next month. There's only nineteen days to go,' Kieran announces.

'You don't really need a comb for every day of the year. One comb can last you a long time,' Sally tells her son.

'Don't be ridiculous. Combs always lose their strength after one day. They're no use to me then.'

'I'll give you your thirty-one combs in nineteen days' time,' I inform Kieran.

'I want them to be brown and all exactly the same.'

'Yes, we're aware of your comb requirements, so don't worry,' I reply.

This comb obsession started about two years ago. I remember looking extensively at the price of combs and some were actually selling for twenty pounds. I mean who buys a twenty pound comb? We managed to find a company that gives us a significant discount due to the volume that we order. It's now around twenty-five pence per comb. We're only into the second week of the month but as we head towards the end of the month Kieran gets increasingly anxious that he won't get a new supply. When we hand over the next batch of combs on the first of the month he looks so relieved.

About six months ago we decided to reduce his anxiety by giving him two months' supply at once but that threw him. He kept kicking the extra box and shouting 'there's too many combs around me and they're ruining my life.' So we reverted back to the month by month intake.

Autism is just so complicated.

I'm sure that Kieran is single-handedly keeping that company afloat.

'Anyway what's the name of this bloke that's my dad's substitute?' Kieran asks Sally.

'His name is Robert.'

'How tall is he?'

'I think he's probably just over six foot.'

'Didn't you know how tall he was before you went off to the Blackburn mountains with him?'

'I'm pretty sure he's six foot one.'

'Does he wear socks?'

'Yes he does.'

'Every single day?'

'Yup.'

'What's his favourite colour?'

'I'm not sure.'

'Does he swim?'

'I don't know.'

'Can he play tennis?'

'I don't think so but I'm not absolutely certain on that.'

'You don't seem to know much about this bloke. What about basketball?'

'I'm pretty confident he can't play basketball.'

'Does he laugh?'

'Yes, sometimes.'

'What makes him laugh?'

'Let me think. Oh yes, the other day we saw a guy who was looking at his mobile walk straight into a lamppost.'

'Did he hurt himself?'

'Well he did hit his head quite hard.'

'So this Robert character laughed because someone got hurt. He sounds a bit of a bastard.'

'Robert is not a bastard, he's a very nice man, hopefully you'll meet him soon.'

'Is he going to laugh at me?'

'Only if you tell him a joke.'

'What about if I fall over and break my leg? Would he laugh his socks off?'

'No he certainly wouldn't. How do you feel about seeing him?'

'If he brings me loads of presents then I suppose it'll be OK but he does sound like a bit of an idiot.'

Sally glances at me with a relieved expression. I'm sure this is the first time that she's had a discussion with her son about the prospect of Kieran meeting Robert. I'm pleased that it looks like he'll be getting another visitor and from what Sally told me Robert sounds like a decent guy so hopefully the meeting will go well but with Kieran that is always so unpredictable.

So that's one potential new visitor for Kieran, now I've got to work on adding another one.

CHAPTER SIXTEEN: SIENNA

Sally did take Kieran out to Sainsbury's and bought him his KitKat before dropping him back here. She left soon afterwards to return to Blackburn.

Just before I head out to meet Ryan I receive a text from the Wimbledon theatre – 'My apologies for the late notice but the Bob Denny performance tomorrow night is cancelled. A full refund will be paid into your bank account within five working days.'

Without hesitation I ring up the theatre.

'Hello, Wimbledon theatre, how can I help you?'

'I've just received a text from you informing me that the Bob Denny gig tomorrow night is cancelled. Why's that?' I ask.

'Unforeseen circumstances I'm afraid.'

'It doesn't make any sense. Cancelling it with less than twenty-four hours to go? I'm a carer in an autistic care home and I was going with one of the residents who is a massive fan of Denny; he's going to be really upset. There must be a valid reason for this?'

'Between you and me it's down to poor ticket sales. We've a capacity for one thousand six hundred and seventy and so far we've only sold eighty-two tickets.

His management were way too ambitious with this one. Although they'll incur a financial loss in pulling out it would've been much worse for them if it went ahead. They should've made this decision much earlier.'

'Yes, I wish that would've happened as I only booked the tickets a couple of days ago.'

'I'm really sorry for the inconvenience.'

'It's OK, it's not your fault. I'm just worried how I'm going to explain it to my guy. He doesn't like plans changing at the best of times, least of all when he's so excited to be going but anyway thanks for explaining it to me, I appreciate it.'

'Good luck.'

Eighty-two tickets? Wow. His stock has really plummeted. Maybe I should write to his manager and suggest a gig at our care home? An audience of five sounds just about his level right now.

All that's left for me to do is to inform Kieran; simple really.

I nervously enter his bedroom. He's actually watching a Bob Denny DVD. I've sat with Kieran watching this DVD a number of times. It's an old performance as Denny still has a full head of hair. Although these days he lets his hair grow long on the sides despite virtually nothing on the top. Not a good look.

'Kieran, do you mind putting that on pause for a minute?' I ask.

'I can't do that, I'm laughing too much.'

'OK, I'm afraid to have to tell you that the show tomorrow is cancelled,' I blurt out, there's no room for small talk.

'Fuck the shit off,' he shouts at me.

At least I've got his attention.

'It's true but hopefully it'll be rescheduled,' I lie.

'Is it because of that joke he told about the horse going into the pub? I told him that was a lump of shit.'

'No, it wasn't because of that.'

'I know, it's that joke about hating the clocks going forward in March cos they always fall off his mantelpiece. I didn't understand that and only three people in the audience laughed.'

'No, it's because they didn't sell many tickets.'

'That's ridiculous, he's the funniest man on this earth and all the other planets too.'

'That's what the theatre told me and I believe them.'

'They're lying cos they don't want us all laughing. I'm destroyed.'

He throws the DVD cover across the room and head-butts the wall with fierce intensity. I attempt to stop him but he forcefully pushes me away.

'Kieran, I understand why you're upset but it's out of our hands. His management cancelled it but we'll book another venue, I promise. We will get to see him,' I say as I approach him but he turns to face me and promptly gives me a hefty head-butt. I see stars and stumble to the floor. He then kicks me in the shins a couple of times so I shout for Mick and John, who are the other male staff members on duty. They arrive straight away and manage to restrain him but his eyes are transfixed on me, he really wants to hurt me.

Mandy appears shortly afterwards with the Lorazepam drug, which will hopefully calm him down pretty quickly. We only use it in emergencies and this is definitely an emergency. With great difficulty she manages to get him to swallow the pill. Kieran desperately tries to break free from Mick and John's grasp but they're too well trained in this type of scenario for him to succeed. Although I feel shaken after his attack I'm still talking to him in a reassuring and calm manner.

It takes around fifteen minutes before he eventually relaxes and the guys let go of him. He then sits at the end of his bed just shaking his head.

'Are you OK?' Mandy asks me.

'I've felt better.'

'What the hell happened?'

'Let's go outside,' I reply, leaving Mick and John to watch over Kieran.

We venture downstairs to the dining room.

'The Bob Denny gig was cancelled. When I told Kieran he absolutely flipped,' I tell Mandy.

'Oh, I see. Did you expect that reaction?'

'I knew that he'd be really disappointed but the intensity of his physical attack was quite shocking.'

'Do you need medical attention?' Mandy asks.

'No, I think I'll have a few bruises on my right shin and my head hurts a bit but I'll be OK. I haven't seen him that bad for quite a while.'

'I wonder if in future when we book these events we don't tell any of the residents until the very last minute just in case.'

'Yeah, you've got a point.'

'Are you sure you're OK?'

'It's just so disappointing to see him revert to the sort of behaviour he exhibited when I first arrived here.'

'So how will you deal with this?'

'When he used to do this to me previously I tried to get him to talk about it, maybe get to the root cause but of course the root cause was always autism, combined with his ADHD. At the end of the day he can't control his actions but right at this moment in time that doesn't help me coping with this situation. I feel very let down as I've made such good progress with him. Although I don't want to see him right now I'll stay here tonight just in case.'

'You don't have to do that. Go home, have a glass of wine and try to relax.'

'No, I can't do that. I'm too worried about him. I feel better if I'm nearby. Mick and John are on duty tonight so between us we'll be able to handle anything that may crop up.'

'I know that he used to spit at you quite a lot but did he ever attack you with that same intensity?'

'Oh yes, especially in the first few months but I really can't remember the last time he hit me.'

'Did he ever apologise?'

'Never. Anyway do you mind popping up to see him? I'm just wondering if there's any injury to his head, I didn't notice anything but if you can just check?'

'Of course. I'm sure the guys would've notified us if he needed any medical attention but I'll let you know how he is.'

'Thanks.'

A few minutes later a text arrives on my mobile, it's from Ryan.

'You're late and the wine I poured out for you is getting warm so I may have to drink it myself.'

'My apologies. Something's cropped up at work that requires my attention. Can we rearrange for the same time tomorrow?' I reply.

'Of course, don't worry. I hope all is OK with you?'

'Yes, everything's fine. Again I'm sorry for the late notice.'

'No problem. I look forward to seeing you tomorrow.'

I didn't want to tell him that his brother just attacked me because that could seriously jeopardise any possible reunion, although seeing how Kieran reacted tonight makes me begin to doubt that getting him and Ryan together is a good idea.

CHAPTER SEVENTEEN:
SIENNA

I awake at four o'clock the following morning. I didn't sleep well as I kept going over and over in my head what happened in Kieran's bedroom. Could I have handled it better? I did just announce the cancellation without any preamble, which might have softened the impact. But I still think he would have reacted badly.

I have a quick wash in the staff bathroom and cautiously make my way upstairs to Kieran's bedroom. He's not a good sleeper at the best of times and given what happened last night I'm pretty confident he's awake.

His door is half opened and the television is on. I gently knock on the door.

'Hello, Kieran, it's only me,' I say, but there's no response.

I warily enter his bedroom. He is sitting on his bed in his pyjamas watching TV.

'Good morning, how are you today?' I ask.

'I feel exactly like that pile of turd that those foxes leave in our garden.'

'Is that because of the Bob Denny cancellation?'

'Of course and I blame you.'

'Like I told you yesterday it has nothing to do with me, it's because they didn't sell enough tickets.'

'That's ridiculous, he could fill out Wembley stadium easily.'

Eighty-two tickets sold as opposed to ninety thousand? I think Kieran's being a trifle optimistic but I won't tell him that as my head and right shin can't take another bashing right now.

'Once another gig is confirmed we'll definitely get tickets,' I try to reassure him. Wherever he's playing next, be it Wembley stadium or our local Wetherspoons pub, I will attempt to get tickets but will only let Kieran know at the last minute to avoid that reaction again.

'Is the reason we didn't go because he has no hair left on the top of his head?' Kieran asks.

'No, it's got nothing to do with his hair loss. I've just told you the reason.'

'Or is it because he smiles too much when he's telling the jokes?'

He's just not getting it.

'Kieran, I know that you were disappointed when I told you yesterday but did you think it was right to head-butt and kick me? You really hurt me.'

He continues to stare at his TV and doesn't respond.

'Should you apologise to me?'

He looks at me and smiles but doesn't say anything. I have no idea if that's his version of an apology but I don't pursue it.

One of the common traits of autism is lack of empathy. The fact that he attacked me so viciously yesterday and hurt me doesn't seem to bother him. His disappointment in not seeing Denny clearly overrides everything.

'OK, I'll leave you be. I hope you have a better day,' I tell Kieran.

'It's going to be another turd day,' he replies.

There were no major incidents throughout the rest of the day. Kieran was very quiet and subdued and there was very little interaction between us. I wonder if any of the other eighty Bob Denny fans who missed out beat someone up in frustration? I'd like to think not but who knows?

I leave the care home by mid-afternoon as I'm still in yesterday's clothes. I return home, have a shower, put on new gear and arrive at Ryan's bang on time.

Before I've even set foot in his flat Ryan has already handed me a nice cold glass of wine, accompanied by a lovely smile. Both are just what I need right now. We take our usual positions in his living-room, Ryan sitting in his armchair and me on the sofa.

'So how's Kieran?' Ryan asks.

'He's fine,' I lie.

'Did your absence yesterday have anything to do with him?'

'No, it was one of the other residents. We all work as a team so when an incident occurs we all muck in,' I lie again. The actual fib is not identifying Kieran as the culprit but the rest of what I said is true. The care home staff all help each other and yesterday's incident was an example of that.

'I spoke to my mum today,' Ryan tells me, seemingly accepting my explanation.

'And how did that go?'

'I asked her why she didn't try to contact me soon after I left home. After all I was only sixteen. I thought she might be a little concerned.'

'What did she say?'

'Basically the same explanation as before – too tied up with Kieran.'

'But I thought that you were relieved to be out of that household and away from all that stress, so why were you bothered?'

'If you asked me that question back then I would've told you I didn't give a toss but I've often reflected on it since and it's festered away at me.'

'Did it help talking to her last night?'

''Yes, I can tell she's genuinely remorseful so I'm finally understanding that we should leave all of that in the past and rebuild our relationship. I never thought that I would ever come to that realisation.'

'I cannot tell you how pleased that makes me feel to hear you say that. You've come a long way in such a short time.'

'And like my mother said when we all met up, this wouldn't have been possible without you. You've been amazing and because I have complete faith in you, I'm now able to finally meet my brother.'

'Wow, that's a surprise,' is all I can say.

'I thought I might get a more enthusiastic response. It's been what you've been after since you first turned up unannounced at my front door.'

'I just didn't expect it so soon. When do you want this to happen?'

'As soon as possible. Just let me know the time and place and I'll be there.'

'OK but before we do that I'll like to delve into your relationship with Kieran in more detail. So far we've mostly talked about your parents.'

'If you think that will help then fine.'

The timing of this is not good. If the last twenty-four hours is anything to go by I have my doubts as to whether this reunion should go ahead, at least not right now.

'So fire away,' he says enthusiastically.

The roles have suddenly been reserved. He's super keen whilst I'm super worried.

'Was there ever a time when you got on with your brother?' I ask.

'At a guess I'd say only in the first few years of his life but again I was way too young to remember that.'

'Do you know when his behavioural issues began?'

'After speaking to Mum today she told that it was when he was three years old so I would've been six. Nearly all my memories of Kieran were of him hitting me and Mum and just generally being very disruptive.'

'Did you know that he was autistic?' I ask.

'Yes. Mum told me when I was about eight but from what I can remember she didn't really go into any detail. I suppose I should've looked it up to get more of an understanding but I just thought that he was a pain in the arse who gave me nothing but grief so I didn't bother.'

'But as you got older didn't you want to know more about autism?'

'No. As I've mentioned to you a few times already I associated Kieran with a very bad time in my life and I just wanted to block out all memories of him.'

'Yet you always sent him birthday and Christmas presents, so you didn't entirely forget about him.'

'No, I suppose not. But sending presents a couple of times a year made me feel less guilty for abandoning him at such a young age. As much as I tried to compartmentalise Kieran my subconscious guilt was never far away. It's complex.'

He takes another sip of wine.

'I did wonder when I posted those presents what his reaction was,' he adds.

'He was always so pleased to get them but he never questioned where they came from. As we've previously discussed, whenever I talked about you to him he told me that you vanished and were the invisible man.'

'Yeah, that just about sums me up.'

'But you've got a chance now to reconnect. It's just the timing has got to be right.'

'What do you mean by that? What's left to discuss about our relationship? Is there a reason why you're thinking of delaying it?'

How can I answer that question without revealing what happened last night? I felt terrible about lying to him earlier and now he needs to know the truth.

'I haven't been entirely honest with you…'

'I don't understand?'

'The incident last night did involve Kieran.'

'Is he OK?'

'Yes, he's fine.'

'But you told me it was one of the other residents so why didn't you tell me the truth?'

'I'm so sorry but I desperately want this reunion to go ahead and I just think there's a chance it won't once I tell you what happened.'

'Just tell me,' he says, looking both worried and irritated.

'Kieran really loves the comedian Bob Denny and we were supposed to see him tonight. However the show was cancelled yesterday afternoon due to poor ticket sales. When I informed Kieran of this he went berserk. He head-butted me and kicked me a number of times so we had the give him the Lorazepam drug that I was telling you about the other day and he soon calmed down. But he still blames me for not going despite being told several times the real reason for the cancellation.'

'Oh my God, that's terrible. Are you OK?' He asks, looking concerned.

'Yes, I'm fine. We're not really on speaking terms right now but I'm sure that'll pass.'

'Why didn't you tell me this when I asked you earlier?'

'I didn't want to put you off seeing your brother. I apologise again for not telling you the truth. So anyway now you know.'

'Has he hit you before?'

'Yes, in the first few months after I was assigned to him but not for a long time. He absolutely hates it whenever a plan is changed so I knew he'd be really disappointed but I didn't expect a physical assault.'

'It's me that should apologise to you. Getting physically abused shouldn't be part of your job description. I'm glad you told me.'

'I suppose this means that the reunion is off?'

'No it doesn't. I'm determined to meet Kieran and will work with you to rebuild my relationship with him. Obviously now isn't the right time but I'm hoping it won't be too long before it is. I know it's a risk that he might regress but if you think that risk is low then I'm up for it'

'Wow, you've surprised me twice tonight.'

'My reunion with my mother has convinced me that I just have to meet Kieran again. Of course it distresses me that he lashed out at you but unfortunately that seems to be the nature of the beast. Before we meet up we need to go through all his issues again and try to avoid any possible trigger points, I'm finally beginning to realise that we need to approach this very carefully. I've blocked Kieran from half of my entire life so I think it's time I made up for all those lost years.'

'I'll try to rebuild his trust in me in the coming days and we'll take it from there.'

'Sounds good. Now can we draw a line on this rather heavy conversation and talk about something else?' He asks.

'OK, what do you want to talk about?'

'A bit personal but why did your last relationship end?' Ryan asks.

'Talk about changing the subject,' I reply.

'I'm sorry. You don't have to answer that.'

'It's not a problem. I can't complain as I've been peppering you with personal questions since we met, although I still don't know too much about your relationships outside your family.'

'You first.'

'His name's Philip. I met him in a pub nearly two years ago. We happened to be ordering our drinks at the same time and got chatting. He's a good looking guy and was quite charming. I was a little surprised that he was taking an interest in me. The following week we went out on our first date. The first eighteen months or so were really good. We went on some spectacular holidays in that short time – Australia, Japan and Malaysia but fundamentally we have different outlooks on life. He's a lawyer and is very career-driven. He is also extremely materialistic. We always went to the best restaurants and exclusive nightclubs which sounds wonderful but after a while the novelty wears off. I remember once suggesting we go to McDonalds for lunch and he just stared at me as if I had committed a murder. We didn't go. Although he never verbalised it, I always got the impression that he thought I could do better in my career, given my university degrees. He never understood that looking after special needs adults was my passion. Whenever I talked to him about my day with Kieran his eyes just glazed over. I knew that there was no future in that relationship and to be honest I'm surprised that it lasted as long as it did.'

'So did you end it?'

'No it was him.'

'And what reason did he give?'

'It all came to a head on the night we were supposed to be seeing Ed Sheeran. He got front row seats which must have cost him a fortune but I had to cancel at the last minute as Kieran was having a bit of a meltdown over something or other. We had a massive argument over the phone. He told me that my job was all-consuming, leaving little time for him.'

'Was there any truth in that?'

'Yes, but he did forget to mention that his job was also very demanding so I could've turned that conversation around but didn't. I was a little hurt at first but now I'm relieved to be out of it. Anyway that's enough about me, tell me a bit more about your liaisons with the ladies.'

'Liaisons with ladies? Have you just finished reading *Pride and Prejudice*?'

'Stop stalling.'

'Being the perceptive person that you are you've already worked out some of the issues I've had with women. The longest I've been in a relationship is nine months and it's nearly always me that breaks it off. I've never cheated on anyone but once the slightest cracks start to appear I jump ship. I'm not proud of doing that, in fact I feel quite ashamed of my behaviour. I know all of this probably doesn't make much sense but that's just the way I feel. As you rightly point out it could all possibly stem back to my fractured relationship with my mother. Or maybe I haven't met the right person yet. Who knows? So really that's my history with the opposite sex in a nutshell.'

'As you're now beginning to resolve some of the issues with your mother do you think that might help with future relationships?'

'Who knows? Only time will tell.'

We spend the next hour or so just chatting and drinking. Despite my news about Kieran he seems determined to meet his brother. Normally I would have been thrilled at this but I have to adopt a cautious approach. The timing has to be right.

I meant to ring Sally today to let her know about yesterday's incident but it's getting late so I'll contact her first thing tomorrow morning. I also need to inform her about Ryan's decision.

Naturally she's bound to be distressed to hear about Kieran and I have no doubt she'll have mixed feelings about her sons meeting again after so many years. She's right to be concerned about the possibility that Kieran may revert to some of his disruptive behaviour.

It's not a conversation that I'm looking forward to.

CHAPTER EIGHTEEN: SIENNA

The walk from the tube station to StarLight gives me the opportunity to talk to Sally without any distractions.

'I really think you should forget about this reunion for now,' Sally tells me after I brought her up to date with everything.

'Sally, I understand your concerns, they're mine too but we can't put this off indefinitely.'

'But that attack on you was such a setback.'

'He doesn't like any change of plans so I'm partly to blame by letting him know that it was all happening. A lesson learned. Nobody likes to be disappointed, we just all handle it differently. I can clearly remember one summer's day when I was about four or five, the family were all going to Brighton for the day and for some reason it got cancelled. I was really gutted, so much so I can vividly recall how I felt on that day twenty or so years later. My mum ran a bath for me and I put my on swimming costume and pretended I was in the sea at Brighton. But guess what? It wasn't quite the same.'

'But why would you risk escalating his bad behaviour?'

'Sally, I'm also guilty of thinking about the worse case scenario but have you ever thought that this might be a happy experience?'

'Maybe it will be, I just don't know. I'm so confused right now.'

'You've got Ryan back in your life and he's now willing to see Kieran; isn't this what you've always wanted?'

'Yes of course but it could all go horribly wrong.'

'Rest assured I'm not going to take any unnecessary risks. Please trust me with this.'

'You know I have one hundred percent faith in you but that still doesn't stop me worrying.'

'When it happens it'll be something to celebrate, having your family back together again. Sally, let me go as I'm on my way in. I'll ring you tonight to let you know how Kieran got on today.'

'Yes please do. I may be further away from him but he's never far from my thoughts.'

I feel slightly anxious as I enter the care home. What mood Kieran is in will determine what sort of day lays ahead of me. Although I've dealt with every Kieran scenario it's been such a long time since he's been so aggressive and it's unnerved me. I'm also beginning to feel under pressure with the possible reunion hanging over my head. Sally and Ryan are relying on me to get this decision right.

Kieran and Jamie are in the living-room watching an Alan Titchmarsh gardening programme.

'Good morning guys,' I say to both of them.

There's no response.

'Do you like Alan Titchmarsh?' I ask.

'His voice is smooth and makes me feel better. It's the exact same feeling I get when I'm eating a bowl of chocolate ice cream,' Jamie replies.

An interesting comparison.

'And what about you, Kieran, do you like Alan Titchmarsh?'

'I like the way he looks at me when he's talking,' he replies. 'Anyway when you were slurping your coffee downstairs I heard you say to Mandy that you've met the invisible man. Is that true?'

'I don't know what you're talking about,' I reply. Although actually I do.

'The person who lived with me and Mum until the twelfth of October 2009. I think he got fed up with me and then pissed off. When I was younger he was my brother and his name is Ryan.'

'Oh, him,' I innocently reply. 'Yes, I've seen him recently.'

'Is he still thin?'

'Yes, but probably more muscular than when you last saw him.'

'Has he still got those bruises on his arm that I gave him?'

'No, they've gone.'

'Is he still wearing those blue underpants? He had loads of them.'

'I don't know.'

'Haven't you seen him in his underpants?'

I shake my head.

I'm keeping my responses to the bare minimum as I'm still in a state of shock with this unexpected development.

'I liked head-butting him cos he had a nice strong head and it made a lovely sound, although he always seemed fed up when I did it.'

'As I said to you yesterday it's not nice to hurt people even when you're angry.'

'But what else should I do?'

'Just go off by yourself and try to chill out. Remember when I taught you those deep breathing exercises? They'll help you to relax and not get so aggressive.'

'That stupid breathing is for bald arseholes.'

'Anyway how would you feel if Ryan came to visit you?' I ask. In for a penny…

'Is he still taller than me?'

'Yes he is.'

'Has he fixed his smiling problem?'

'What do you mean?'

'He never smiled in my house. I think he went to the doctor about it.'

That visit was probably due to his anxiety.

'He definitely smiles now.'

'Is he applying to be my brother for the second time?'

'He's always been your brother. Remember the presents that always arrived for your birthday and Christmas? Well Ryan sent those. You enjoyed getting those presents, didn't you?'

'There was always too much Sellotape on the boxes. I don't like the Sellotape noise, my teeth hurt when I had to destroy the Sellotape.'

'But Ryan just wanted to make sure that the presents arrived safely. So would you like to see your brother again?' I ask again.

'Yeah, that's a good idea. I can tell him not to put loads of Sellotape on those boxes. That'll make me feel calmer.'

Wow, that was easy, well apart from fielding questions on Ryan's weight, height, bruises, underpants and use of Sellotape.

I can't believe that this will actually happen. Of course I'm under no illusions that it could still go pear-shaped but the fact that he's actually agreed to meeting his brother is a major step forward.

I won't pursue this conversation as a decision has been made and I'm afraid that if I continue to talk about it he'll change his mind. I'll ring both Sally and Ryan later when I get the opportunity. I'm curious to see what their initial reactions will be. But for now I just want to have a nice day with Kieran. I won't mention the Bob Denny incident again as he's made his mind up as to who was responsible.

'I really like dressing gowns,' Kieran announces, the master of random statements.

'Why's that?' I ask.

'There's no buttons, but I never see anyone wearing them on the streets.'

'Dressing gowns are normally worn indoors, mainly before or after a shower.'

'Is that a Government law?'

'No, it's not, but you don't usually see people walking around outside in their dressing gown or pyjamas, do you?'

'But when we went to Sainsbury's on the nineteenth of October last year we saw an old geezer at a bus stop in his pyjamas, smoking four cigarettes at once and he was dancing. That guy was fantastic.'

Fantastic? That's debatable. I would imagine that most members of the public would regard the cigarette man as completely off his trolley but as a carer for adults with mental health issues I have to modify that description. Let's just say I think he's eccentric.

'He's the exception,' I diplomatically reply.

'Do you like hair?'

'Like the hair on your head?' I ask.

'Any hair.'

'Some people have nice hair styles whilst others I don't really care for. It's all about individual tastes.'

'Do you like your own hair?'

'It's OK. Maybe I could do with a hair cut right now.'

'It looks ridiculous. It goes down to your shoulders and I haven't seen your ears when we're indoors for the last fifty-nine weeks. Your hair also waves around too much whenever it's a bit windy. When it's not windy your hair still irritates me but when that wind blows up I want to get a scissors and cut it all off.'

This comes as no surprise to me as we've had this exact same conversation many times previously.

'I like shorter hair but just long enough so I can comb it. Just like Naga Munchetty's. I don't like bald people, they're pricks with no brains inside of them.'

'OK, changing a subject, Miriam rang me this morning, she was wondering if you'd like to pop down to her shop for an informal chat.'

Miriam works for a private charity called Full of Heart which raises donations for heart patients in local hospitals. Her shop sells second hand books, clothes, DVDs etc. It's only a few minutes' walk from the care home and as I walked past it recently I saw an advertisement for volunteers which made me think that it would be a really good working experience for Kieran. I discussed it with Sally and she thought that it was an excellent opportunity for her son. Kieran, like all the other residents here, has never worked. We agreed that it could be a real confidence booster for him and could even lead to paid employment. When I suggested this to him he said he'd think about it. He's been thinking about it for the last sixteen days.

'What do I have to do in this goddamn shop?' Kieran asks.

'When the second hand clothes, books and DVDs arrive you sort them out and put them on display so that people can buy them.'

'Hold on, did you say second hand clothes?'

'Yes, people donate them to the heart charity that Miriam runs.'

'So does that mean I have to pick up someone else's shitty underpants and put them in the shop window?'

'I don't think anyone will send in their underpants.'

Hopefully not anyway.

'Those people who buy these clothes must be losers or a bit mad.'

'Not everyone can afford new clothes.'

'But how much does a pair of underpants cost?'

'Can we get off the subject of underpants please? Let's just go down and see Miriam and then you can ask her all of these type of questions yourself.'

'What sort of hair has this Miriam person got?'

'You'll be pleased to know that she has short hair. Actually it looks a bit like Naga Munchetty's.'

He immediately goes into his bedroom and puts on his jacket. I just knew that referring to Naga's hair would be a deal breaker.

CHAPTER NINETEEN: SIENNA

Five minutes later we arrive at Miriam's charity. She invites us into her office. She's a very attractive woman, probably in her mid-forties, tall, with long toned legs and, of course, short stylist hair. Kieran is just staring at her hair and smiling. I should have warned Miriam about Kieran's obsession.

'So what do you know about Full of Heart?' Miriam asks Kieran.

'You sell clothes that people have been wearing for years and they want to get rid of them cos they stink.'

'Not quite. With all the clothes that are kindly donated to us we decide if they are in good enough condition to sell and if they're not but still OK to wear we give them to a couple of the local homeless charities.'

'You mean those drunks who live in Finsbury Park and smell like shit?'

'What might be a good idea, if you're agreeable to it, is if you spend some time with the Full of Heart team when we visit the homeless. Most of them are good people who have had some traumatic event happen in their lives that led them to sleeping rough. I think it'll be a good experience for you.'

'No way, I don't want to get any diseases from those arseholes.'

Miriam looks over at me but I shake my head to indicate not to pursue this conversation. Maybe this is something I can work on with Kieran? His autism determines that he has fixed ideas on certain aspects of life which heavily restricts his wider understanding of the world around him. It won't be easy but it's giving me food for thought.

Although Miriam is not experienced with autism and all of its complicated behaviours she's clever enough to cut short the conversation on the homeless. Even though I've been dealing with autistic adults for the past three years I am nowhere near fully understanding all of its complexities.

I'd like to meet the person who is.

'But with the clothes that are in good condition we always wash them before putting them on the shop floor.' Miriam adds.

'Do I have to talk to the customers? I don't like chatting to strangers. You're OK cos you've got short hair.'

Miriam looks a trifle confused at that last remark but doesn't question his logic. She's learning fast.

'We'll train you on the tills so at the very least you have to tell the customer the item cost and thanking them for their purchase.'

'Why do I need to thank them?'

'It's just being polite. We've had many discussions on this,' I add.

'But I only want to talk to you, Mum, Jamie, Billy, Nicky and short-haired people. I'm not getting involved in these stranger's lives.'

'Kieran you can't go through life only talking to a handful of people,' I say.

'Why not?'

'You can learn so much from other people.'

'As long as I can watch my DVDs and walk on the Finsbury Park grass I'm not interested in anything else.'

This 'interview' is going off on tangents and I'm not sure if Miriam quite knows what she's getting herself into but to her credit she doesn't seem to be too fazed by Kieran's comments.

'OK, we won't let you serve the customers until you're ready. How do you feel about that?' Miriam asks Kieran.

'That's better but how many bank notes are you going to give me for sorting out all those underpants?'

'As it's voluntary work we can't pay you but we can supply you with as much tea and biscuits as you like,' Miriam replies, smiling.

'That's just ridiculous. I'm outta here.'

With that he literally runs out of the shop.

As Kieran is not too clued up on road safety I run after him and just as he's about to dash across a busy side road I manage to grab his jacket and pull him back to safety.

A car screeches to a halt.

'What the fuck are you doing you arsehole?' The driver shouts at Kieran.

'I'm not an arsehole but I have met a few and I don't like them,' Kieran replies.

The man looks perplexed, shakes his head and speeds off.

'Kieran, what did I tell you about crossing the road?' I ask.

'But I want to get back to StarLight quickly.'

'You were just about to run out in front of that car, you could've been hurt.'

'Nah, they would've stopped.'

How can he be so supremely confident in a driver's ability to stop on a dime is beyond me.

'Please don't rush out onto road again,' I tell him.

'But I didn't cos you stopped me. You were just being a spoilsport.'

A spoilsport? That's the thanks I get for saving him from serious injury or worse.

We walk across the road and a few minutes later we're back at StarLight.

'Kieran, remember the other day when we had that session about being rude?'

'No, I wasn't paying attention to that shit.'

'Can you tell me how you were rude to Miriam just now?'

'I was nice to the short haired lady.'

'For a start didn't you tell her that you don't want to get a disease from the homeless?'

'What's wrong with that?' He innocently asks.

'We'll discuss that later but when she told you that voluntary workers don't get paid you just ran out of her store without saying anything to her.'

'She's a con artist. Just giving her employees tea and biscuits instead of wages? She must think I'm an imbecile.'

'Kieran, let me try to explain. Miriam runs an organisation to raise money for people suffering with heart conditions.'

'So me selling the dirty underpants will cure all those people in hospitals with crap hearts?' He asks with no hint of sarcasm.

Once Kieran gets a bee in his bonnet (i.e underpants) he doesn't let it go.

'The clothes, books, DVDs etc all raise donations for heart patients. It gives them financial support when they're recovering from heart operations. A lot of these patients have issues getting paid if they have lengthy sick leave so Miriam's charity helps them cope financially. Nearly all employees who work for various charities do it voluntarily and therefore don't get paid. They just want to help people recover from their health issues without worrying about being able to pay the bills. Miriam is definitely not trying to con anybody. Do you understand what I just said?'

'Yes, she gets everyone to work for biscuits to help people who are going to die.'

'No not quite. It's for people recovering from illness. Hopefully they'll be ok. I think that this will be a good opportunity for you to gain work experience and maybe help you to get a paid job sometime in the future.'

'Do they sell any *Friends* DVDs?'

'I would think so.'

'OK, if Miriam can give me a *Friends* DVD as a bonus I'll make sure that all those ill people with shitty hearts get better. But I've got series one, two and three so it has to be series four or else I'm not interested.'

'OK, it's a deal. I'll contact Miriam and we'll work out what days she wants you to work.'

'And tell her I need chocolate digestive biscuits as well.'

'I will, no problem.'

Kieran is a hard negotiator. Series four of *Friends* and chocolate digestive biscuits. I wonder if your average Premier League footballer requests a similar signing on bonus when negotiating a new contract?

I order series four of *Friends* on Amazon straight away. I then ring Miriam and apologise on Kieran's behalf (not that he gives a toss) for his abrupt exit but she laughs it off and we agree that Kieran will start working one day a week, starting from next Monday. We also decided that I would stay with him throughout the day just in case of any issues.

After the stress of the last couple of days I now feel so much better after Kieran secured the voluntary work position and of course the news that Sally's two sons will eventually meet up after so many years apart. There's no better time to ring Sally.

'Hi, Sienna. Is everything OK?' She anxiously asks. This is her normal greeting on phone calls as if she expects to hear bad news every time I ring her. Well today it is quite the reverse.

'Yes, it's all good. First of all Kieran met Miriam this morning and whilst it wasn't the most straightforward of interviews she wants him to start work next Monday, one day a week for now.'

'Wow, that's amazing. She must be a very special lady to take on my boy.'

'She is and that was after some typical Kieran behaviour which I'll tell you about in a minute.'

I wonder how many interviewees that ran out in the middle of the interview still get the job?

'But even more important than that is that Kieran wants to meet Ryan.'

'You're kidding me?'

'No, I'm not. Given Kieran's unpredictable behaviour recently I wasn't going to broach the Ryan subject but he overheard me talking to a colleague about it and that led into a discussion. And he agreed to meet his brother.'

'Without any hesitation?'

'Well he wanted to know if he still had the bruises on his arms from when Ryan was sixteen and asked about Ryan's height, weight and his blue underpants.'

'Sounds like Kieran. I just can't believe it. So when is this going to happen?'

'I've been so busy that I haven't had a chance to speak to Ryan but I'll contact him shortly and hopefully we'll fix a date. Do you want to be there?'

'Yes I would but will that be too much of an overload for Kieran to handle?'

'I'm sure it'll be OK but let me see what Ryan's take on it is.'

'You really are a miracle worker, Sienna, we all owe you so much.'

'You owe me nothing. I just want to see you back as a family again. I'm under no illusions that it'll all go smoothly but I'll be with both your sons every step along the way to help resolve any issues that may occur.'

'You're still so positive even after he attacked you so brutally.'

'Believe me I've cursed your son under my breath many times but I truly love him and I just want to improve the quality of his life. Today he managed to get a job and agreed to see his brother again. That's what I call a good day.'

'Totally agree. Please phone me after speaking to Ryan. I'm excited but also nervous.'

'Perfectly understandable. Rest assured I'll definitely ring you.'

So now onto Ryan. I tried ringing him but there's no reply. He's probably busy at work so I text him.

'Any chance of seeing you tonight?'

An hour later the reply arrives.

'Of course but rather than coming around to mine do you fancy going out for a meal?'

'That'll be great. I'll let you choose the restaurant but I only have one condition - it has to be Italian.'

'I know just the place.'

He signs off his message with a kiss. That's the first time he's done that. I must admit I've grown rather fond of him, he's a lovely bloke who has been through a lot, especially when he was younger. I get the impression that he likes me too but I'm useless at picking up romantic signals. Would it be a little too close to home if my relationship with Ryan developed into something deeper? I'm not sure if there's any rule preventing me from dating a brother of one of the residents but I'm getting ahead of myself here. I'm going to the restaurant to tell Ryan the news that Kieran would like to see him. It's not a date, it's strictly a work related meeting, albeit with alcohol, Italian food and a rather good looking guy.

CHAPTER TWENTY:
SIENNA

The rest of the day passes without Kieran mentioning Ryan which is a relief as I'd hate to inform Sally that Kieran had changed his mind.

Ryan is already at the restaurant when I arrive. He looks smarter than his usual casual appearance - clean shaven, a nicely ironed white shirt and he's even wearing a navy blue jacket. I'm slightly underdressed with my jeans and t-shirt but due to my heavy work load today I didn't have time to go home and get changed.Ryan gets up and gives me a hug which isn't the first time he's done this but he holds onto me a bit longer this time.

'This place looks fab,' I remark.

'I think you'll like the food.'

That probably means he's been here before. I was going to ask him that but it might come across as probing, an attempt to find out who he came here with, which is actually what I would like to know.

'So how's my brother?'

'I have news. This morning I asked him if he'd like to see you and he said he would.'

'Oh my God, it's actually going to happen.'

'I certainly hope so. You look shocked. Please don't tell me that you're backing out now?'

'No, I'm desperate to see him, it's just all of these emotions of the last God knows how many years have suddenly hit me, knowing that I'll see him again. It's both a joyful emotion mixed with great anxiety. I don't know if that makes any sense to you.'

'Of course it does. It's an emotional roller coaster for you but please don't get too worked up about it. I'll guide you through it. We won't take any unnecessary risks.'

Before I've got a chance to study the menu Ryan stands up.

'I just want to pop outside for a cigarette. I won't be long.'

Despite my reassurance he still looks anxious. The realisation that this reunion is finally taking place obviously has him worried.

He returns after only a few minutes.

'I didn't know you smoked,' I say.

'I haven't for nearly a decade but after you told me the news I blagged a fag off the waiter.'

'Did it help?'

'Not really, but I only took a few puffs.'

'So the question I have to ask again is are you absolutely sure you still want this to happen? As you know he's been quite challenging recently but I've had a good day with him so if he continues with this good behaviour there's no reason not to do this sooner rather than later; it's entirely your call.'

'Can you give me a few minutes to get used to this please?' He asks.

'I'm sorry, I didn't mean to pressurise you.'

'You really are a dog with a bone,' he says, smiling.

'I have another question.'

'How come that doesn't surprise me?'

'Do you want your mother there when it eventually happens?'

'I don't know, I just don't know…'

'OK, I'll drop the subject now. Let's talk about something else,' I say but I get no response.

'What about films? Are you a film buff?' I ask.

'I love films. I go to the cinema most weeks.'

'OK, a question that I've been askcd a few times before, usually by one of boyfriends, have you got a favourite film?'

'That's easy, *It's A Wonderful Life*.'

'I've never seen it.'

'You're kidding me? I thought everyone in the world had seen that film.'

'Apparently not. Ironically I do love Christmas films.'

'It's a surprisingly dark film and James Stewart is just amazing in it. How he never won an Oscar for that role beggars belief. I've got it on DVD, we should watch it together.'

'A Christmas film in February?'

'It's so much more than a Christmas film, it's about restoring your faith in human nature. I can't wait for you to see it.'

'Talking about that film has definitely shifted your mood; it must be some film.'

'So what's your favourite film?' He asks me.

'I don't really have one.'

'OK, just tell me some of the films that you've really liked,' he asks me.

'*One Flew Over The Cuckoos Nest*, *Schindler's List*, *Manhattan*, *Annie Hall*…'

'You're a Woody Allen fan?'

'Oh yeah, I love all his films. I just think he's so underrated.'

'Me too. He's amazingly talented. Maybe we should have a Woody Allen film night?'

'Is that before or after *It's A Wonderful Life*?'

'After of course,' he replies, smiling.

'What do you recommend?' I ask, looking at the menu.

'The pasta with red source is delicious and the meatballs are the best you'll have.'

'Is that what you're having?'

'Yeah, every time I come here.'

'So what do you do in your spare time?' Ryan asks, after ordering our meals.

'When I was with Philip we were always going to the theatre, concerts, pubs and restaurants, it was pretty hectic, but since we've split up I've done nothing.'

'OK, before Philip came on the scene what did you do outside work hours?'

'Drawing. Art was my favourite subject at school. It's my passion.'

'Wow, that's fantastic. What do you like to draw?'

'Anything really. A couple of years ago I drew a portrait of my father. He was in tears when I gave it to him. It's hanging in his living-room.'

'I'd love to see it.'

'Maybe one day you will.'

'Did you do one for your mother?' He asks.

'No, not yet.

'You're closer to your father, aren't you?'

'I suppose so. When Mum left to live with the guy she had the affair with I stayed with Dad. I can clearly remember how heartbroken he was. He just looked so sad but he never once bad mouthed my mum in front of me and to all intents and purposes he became a single parent. He's amazing.'

'Thanks for sharing that,' Ryan replies, smiling.

We spend the hour eating, drinking and chin-wagging about everything apart from Kieran.

'Fancy coming up for another drink?' He asks as we arrive outside his flat.

'Sorry, I've got to be up early tomorrow but thanks so much for the lovely meal, the food was excellent, as was the company.'

'And vice versa,' he replies.

'Anyway I better get going.'

We embrace. These hugs are getting increasingly intense. As we pull apart he's looking intently at me but doesn't say anything. I smile at him and head off towards the tube station.

'Aren't you going to ask me about my thoughts on meeting my brother?' He shouts as I'm walking away.

'I thought that subject matter was banned for tonight?'

'The ban has just been lifted. I definitely want to meet Kieran and would also like my mother there too.'

'Are you sure?'

'Absolutely certain. Can you try to arrange it as soon as possible?'

'I'll ring Sally tomorrow and we'll arrange a date. All being well it'll be within the next two to three days but just to warn you that it may not go smoothly, especially initially, so be prepared for that.'

'I'm as nervous as hell but it's something I should've done a long time ago.'

CHAPTER TWENTY ONE: RYAN

Although we shared a bottle of wine over dinner it won't be enough to get me to sleep tonight so the first thing I do when inside my flat is pour myself another white wine. When Sienna told me about the prospect of meeting my brother I felt a tightness in my chest and an overwhelming feeling to get sick. Luckily after some comforting words from her those feelings eased but now alone in my flat my anxiety levels are rising again but what's the worse that can happen? Will Kieran start attacking me again and revert back to his old behaviours? If that's the case I'd have to break off any renewed relationship with him and perhaps never see him again. Despite my reluctance in seeing my brother for so many years the thought of not being able to see him again for the rest of my life frightens me.

The fact that my mother's reunion went well has got to give me some hope but then again Kieran's personal circumstances are far more complicated. We're dealing with an adult whose behaviour is unpredictable at best. Without stating the bleeding obvious, his thought process is significantly different from mostly everyone else. Whenever I visualise a positive outcome to this a negative thought always seems to override it. Before Sienna first rang my front door bell it just never occurred to me that I could possibly be reunited with my mother and brother. I always thought that ship has passed but it now looks like within the next couple of days I will eventually see Kieran as an adult for the first time. From reading up on various autism articles and from my conversations with Sienna I cannot expect a tearful reunion. I almost certainly won't get a hug off him, in fact a head-butt would seem more likely and I've got to be prepared for that.

Thank God I have Sienna to guide me on this. I am one hundred percent confident that her astute judgment and risk assessment will determine the most appropriate time to do this. I am completely indebted to this woman and if I'm honest my feelings for her have grown in recent weeks. That dipstick of a boyfriend must be a simpleton. Not only is she a stunning looking woman, she is also kind, thoughtful and has positively changed Kieran's life. Even when I threw a wobbly tonight she took it in her stride and despite the massive effort she has undertaken to get us all to this point she didn't get annoyed with me, quite the reverse. She perfectly understood it from my perspective. The fact that she didn't mention Kieran again for the rest of the evening speaks volumes.

And although my brother wasn't directly involved, he has brought me into contact with Sienna and for that I'll be forever grateful to him.

CHAPTER TWENTY TWO:
SIENNA

'So what country in the world would you like to visit and why?' I ask the group of Kieran, Jamie and Billy.

'Well you didn't want me to go to Hitler's country,' Kieran immediately replies.

'It's not Hitler's country, it's Germany, and I don't think there's too many people that live in Germany who feel proud of Hitler's association with their country.'

'Why not?' He replies.

'He was responsible for the Second World War which resulted in millions of fatalities. We talked about this the other day.'

'But I like his moustache. It's a short one. I don't see many people with short moustaches.'

'Probably because they don't want to look like Hitler.'

'I've seen a few videos of him and he was very excitable. I like that.'

Excitable? I can think of other adjectives to describe him.

'Did his moustache make him an influencer?'

'Can we drop this subject matter now please?' I tell Kieran.

I feel that I should do a history lesson on the Second World War. It probably won't make any difference to Kieran's viewpoint on Hitler as he seems primarily obsessed with his moustache and his exuberant nature but I think I'll do it all the same.

'So what other country would you like to visit?' I ask Kieran.

'Only countries that speak English, like England for example. If I wanted a packet of skittles in Chile how the hell would the bloke in the sweet shop understand what I'm saying? Why doesn't every country just speak English?'

'English is the universal language but most countries have their own language as well,' I say.

'But do they have skittles in Chile?' Kieran asks.

'Yeah, good point. I only want to visit countries that have Skittles, McCoys crisps, Mars Bars and Flakes. If they don't have all of that lot then I know it's a shit country and I'm not getting involved,' Jamie chips in.

'But each country will have their own locally made sweets which I'm sure you'd like,' I add.

'Nah, they'll be shit so I'm staying in Finsbury Park,' Kieran says.

I can see this conversation is going down a cul-de-sac so I'll change the subject.

'What about sports? What's your favourite sport?' I ask the group.

'Don't like any of them,' Kieran replies.

'There must be one you like?'

'Nah.'

'What about you, Jamie. I saw you watching American football the other day on Sky Sports. Do you like American football?'

'No, it's too silly.'

'Then why were you watching it?'

'I like the American accent. It makes me feel good.'

'But when I asked about what countries you'd like to visit you didn't mention America. Would you like to go there?'

'No.'

'Why not?'

'I don't like all the queuing up to get on the aeroplanes and there's too many people on them. I'd like all the Americans to come to England instead.'

I nod as if I understand Jamie's logic but I don't. From my dealings with the autistic adults they all seem completely disinterested in sports but I still try in vain to encourage them to participate in something as I know the exercise is beneficial; so far I haven't succeeded.

'OK, shall we go for a walk to the shops?' I ask.

They all smile and nod as they know this will ultimately result in them receiving goodies.

'Kieran, can I just have a quick word with you please?' I ask as Jamie and Billy leave the room to get their coats.

'How do you feel if Ryan comes to see you tomorrow or Thursday?'

'Will he bring me any presents?'

'Yes he will.'

'With no Sellotape?'

'Of course not.'

'OK, can we go to the shops now?'

I nod. Well that was easier than I expected. Sally and her two sons will finally be reunited but will it be a happy gathering? It won't be long before we find out.

CHAPTER TWENTY THREE: RYAN

'What do I say to him?' I ask Sienna as I make my way to the same restaurant that Sienna and I frequented last week.

'Ryan, you don't have to follow a script, just be yourself and you'll be fine. Did you bring the presents?'

'Yes, everything on your list.'

'And no Sellotape?'

'No wrapping involved. What mood is he in?'

'Calm and particularly looking forward to the pizza.'

'Has he mentioned me at all?'

'No and I'm not going to push it.'

'Is Mum on her way?'

'Yeah, just got a text from her, she's there already.'

'Can Kieran hear our conversation?'

'No, he's got his headphones on listening to the history of British steam engine trains from 1880 to 1901. He's got the hardback in his room as well as the audio version. He doesn't go anywhere without one or the other.'

'Can't say I've seen that one on the best sellers list.'

'It's a specialised subject matter, appealing mostly to the autistic adult community. How long before you get there?'

'Just a few minutes.'

'I'll be there in about ten. I'll see you then but please don't panic, it'll all be OK.'

So within ten minutes I'll be seeing Kieran again. I wonder how much he will remember about our fractured time together? I am hoping that the ton of presents that I've got for him will break the ice. I've no idea how Kieran is feeling right now. Is he as anxious as I am?

My mother is already sitting at the table when I arrive at the restaurant. As I approach her she gets up and gives me a hug. I can tell from the tightness of the embrace that she also feels nervous.

'Shall we get a drink before they arrive?'

She nods.

'I've dreamt of this moment so many times over the years but I just don't know what he'll say or do when he sees you,' she says.

'Neither do I but we just have to play it by ear,' I reply, sounding more confident that I actually feel.

The waiter brings us over our wine and we sit in silence for a few minutes before Sienna and Kieran enter the restaurant.

I didn't know what to expect when I saw my brother again but I feel overcome with emotion. He's a handsome man, with striking blue eyes. He's wearing a smart white shirt and grey trousers. If it wasn't for his autism he'd have no problems attracting the opposite sex. I immediately feel guilty thinking that way. My head is spinning right now. He's looking intently at the other diner's meals and flapping his hands, presumably excited at the prospect of his forthcoming meal.

'How are you, Kieran?' I ask as he approaches the table.

'Did you get the presents?' He replies.

'Yes I did.' I hand a carrier bag full of presents over to him.

'Is the Harry Potter Lego set in there?'

'Yes it is.'

'What about the Jennifer Aniston DVD *Along Comes Polly*?'

'Yeah, they're all in the bag. You can check them out.'

'This is a restaurant, it's not a present opening location. What about the *Glass Cutting For Dummies* book?'

'Yep,' I nod.

'And the thousand piece steam engine train travelling in Lancashire?'

'That was a little more difficult to purchase but I eventually got it.'

A few weeks ago Sienna gave me the heads up on the type of presents that Kieran has recently requested which gave me time to look for the more obscure presents.

'I hope you enjoy them all,' I tell my brother.

'I only enjoy grass but all of this lot will stop me thinking about grass in the evenings.'

'Why don't you thank Ryan?' Sienna asks Kieran.

He doesn't respond to her and sits down next to his mother and then promptly spits into her face. I find this quite shocking but Mum just wipes her face with a tissue and gives Kieran a kiss. I'm finally beginning to realise what she went through for all those years and my admiration for her has increased more than I ever thought possible.

I sit opposite Kieran while Sienna grabs a chair next to me. Kieran hands the carrier bag to Sienna and studies the menu.

'Do you like pizza?' I ask him.

He doesn't reply.

Sienna places her hand on mine and shakes her head. I'm assuming this indicates not to disturb him while he studies the menu.

'There's seven different pizza options which confuses me. I just want a pizza without any of the shit thrown on top of it.'

'I think you want a Margherita, I'll order it for you,' I say.

'What moron piles all that crap on a normal pizza?' Kieran remarks.

I was going to order a pepperoni pizza but at the risk of upsetting my brother I'll get a Margherita instead.

After concurring with my mother and Sienna I order four Margherita pizzas, a coke for Kieran and a bottle of white wine for the three of us, although the way I'm feeling right now I could polish off that bottle by myself.

'It's been a while since we've seen each other,' I say to Kieran.

'Monday October the twelfth 2009 when you vanished into thin air.'

'I'm impressed that you remembered that date,' I nervously reply.

He doesn't respond.

'So how have you been keeping?' I ask.

Again, no reaction.

'Kieran, tell Ryan what's it like at StarLight,' Mum says.

'StarLight is situated at Thornhill Road. It's a three minute walk from Finsbury Park tube station. I have three other friends who stay there and Sienna is my care worker. In the summer she wears shorts and t-shirts that expose her arms and she always keeps her hair long even though she knows that it drives me crazy. She smiles a lot and takes me out for walks in Finsbury Park cos I love being surrounded by grass. A few weeks ago she took me, Jamie and Nicky to a Peter Pan pantomime but it was utter shit as Peter Pan can't fly and when I confronted Pan about that they chucked us out of the theatre cos I told him the truth. On Monday I'm going to start working for some place called Full of Heart. My job is to sell shitty underpants to the Finsbury Park customers so that people who have pathetic hearts won't kick the bucket. Twelve days ago Sienna stopped me from seeing Bob Denny cos she didn't want me to have a laugh.'

'That's a pretty good summary,' Mum tells him.

'I agree,' adds Sienna. 'Ryan, why don't you tell Kieran a bit about yourself?'

'OK, when I left…'

My mother and Sienna both stare at me intently, silently pleading with me not to continue. I take their point. Telling the brother I haven't seen in over fourteen years what I did immediately after deserting him and my mother is perhaps not the smartest way to start off this conversation.

'I'm a plumber and twelve months ago I started my own business. I employ one guy, his name is Robert.'

'Is it Robert Redford, that old actor?' Kieran asks but he's looking at our mother rather than me.

'No, his name is Robert Allison,' I reply.

'Never heard of him but I like Robert Redford. He was in the film *Butch Cassidy And The Sundance Kid.*

I've seen that film six times. Paul Newman is also in that film but he's dead,' Kieran replies again looking at our mother.

'Why do you like grass so much?' I ask.

'That's none of your business,' Kieran replies. This time he is looking at me but with gritted teeth.

For the next few minutes there's silence. I don't think any of us want to follow up on that last remark as it has the potential to escalate. I feel like I'm walking on eggshells right now.

'Where's that fucking pizza?' Kieran shouts. All the nearby diners glance at us.

'It'll be here soon, don't worry,' Sienna replies in her calm and controlled manner.

'But everyone's eating their meals and we're not.'

'That's because they got here before us and ordered their meals before we arrived,' Sienna again explains.

'Are you lying to me again?'

'Why don't we go over to the waiter and ask for an update?' Sienna suggests.

He nods. Kieran and Sienna approach the same waiter who took our order.

'Excuse me, we ordered four pizzas a short time ago but could you let us know approximately when will they be served?' Sienna calmly asks.

'Should be ready within five minutes,' he replies.

'But I need to eat right now,' Kieran pleads.

'It does take a bit of time to cook,' the waiter explains.

'Where is that damn chef? He deserves a head-butt.'

'OK, that won't be necessary. Let's go back to our table,' Sienna tells Kieran.

I heard that conversation and find Kieran's aggressive reaction unsettling and by the look on my mother's face

I'm guessing she feels the same. As Kieran settles back at our table, Sienna goes back to the waiter. This time I can't hear what she's saying to him but I'm assuming she's explaining to him about Kieran's autism and suggesting prioritising his meal and sure enough within a couple of minutes the waiter arrives with a Margherita pizza. Kieran doesn't thank the waiter after receiving his meal and although we're still waiting for ours he starts eating. I'm guessing that social niceties are not a priority for him.

Just as Kieran is finishing his meal ours arrive.

'Can we go now?' I want to get back to see *The Chase*,' Kieran says.

'Once we finish our meals we'll leave,' Sally tells her son.

Kieran shakes his head.

'Bradley Walsh is a funny guy, isn't he?' I say.

Again, no response.

'Do you want some of my pizza?' I ask.

'That's ridiculous. I don't want to catch your germs.'

At least I get a response this time. I'm simply not getting through to him at all. The few times he has acknowledged me his comments have been cutting and aggressive. I'm beginning to feel that he resents me for what I did so long ago but it's too risky to bring that up right now. Sienna did warn me that the initial meeting could be problematic and she was right. I'm eating this pizza way too fast because if I'm being honest I just want to get out of this situation as soon as possible. I occasionally glance at Kieran and notice that his arms are folded and he's tapping his foot impatiently. *The Chase* is obviously a lot more appealing than talking to me.

'How about telling Ryan what your favourite hobbies are?' Mum asks Kieran.

'Grass,' he replies after a lengthy silence.

I'm not sure grass counts as a hobby but it's more than my life's worth to make that point right now.

'OK, that's a start, what else?' Mum says.

'Crisps.'

'What about going for walks, you like that, don't you?'

'Only if it's a KitKat walk.'

'Is KitKat your favourite chocolate?' I ask.

For only the second time this evening Kieran looks at me and again through gritted teeth. He tightens his fists and I'm anticipating a retaliatory punch but instead he starts to bang his own head with his fist. Sienna stops him but only after several blows.

'It's time to go,' Sienna says, looking at Mum who nods.

'Ryan, can you pay the bill and I'll settle with you later?' Sienna says but before I can answer she leaves the restaurant with Kieran. My mother follows them leaving me with three unfinished pizzas and a carrier bag full of presents.

That's not what I call a successful reunion.

CHAPTER TWENTY FOUR:
SIENNA

'Why did you get so angry?' I ask Kieran as we make our way back to StarLight.

'Has that chef cooked pizza before?'

'I'm almost certain he has.'

'Then why did it take him so long? Was he watching *Countdown* instead?'

'I don't understand why you were so nasty to Ryan. He's your brother and you haven't seen him for so long.'

'But he wanted me to open up the presents at the restaurant, that's just ridiculous.'

'OK, if you didn't want to open your presents there you could've at least thanked him and opened them up at the home.'

'But now he's kept them all for himself.'

'No he hasn't. We forgot them and the next time we see him he'll hand them back to us.'

'Of course he won't. He was just pretending to give them to me.'

Despite working with autistic adults for a few years, I'm often flummoxed by their thought process.

'Let's forget about the presents for now. Ryan was very welcoming to you but you were clenching your teeth whenever he asked you a question. Why did you do that?'

'Who approves his brother application?' Kieran asks.

'There is no application, Ryan has always been your brother and always will be,' Sally adds.

'I absolutely loved pinching his arms, legs and face. He did get angry with me but he never hit me back. Not once. Brothers should always hit back.'

'Did you want him to hit you back?' Sally asks.

'Yes of course.'

'But he showed what a loving brother he was by not retaliating. You're very lucky to have him as a brother,' Sally tells Kieran. I can see tears rolling down her cheeks. It's been an emotional evening.

'But you still haven't explained why you got so angry,' Sally asks.

'He wasn't at home from the twelfth of October 2009 so I haven't been able to pinch or head butt him so instead I had to double my punches and head butts to Mum.'

'And that made you feel bad?' Sienna asks.

'He shouldn't have let Mum take all the hits and Mum's arms and legs are thinner so I couldn't grab as much skin. That really pissed me off.'

Sally takes a tissue and wipes her eyes. I'm guessing this is the first time she's heard this confession.

'I had to fulfil my quota of punches and head butts. He must've known that when he buggered off.'

'Kieran, Ryan was too stressed out with the whole family situation. He couldn't handle it and that's why he left. He needed some breathing space. He was more upset with me because I didn't pay him enough attention and he was absolutely right. So please don't blame him for something that happened so long ago. He loves you and always has, the proof of that is he sends you birthday and Christmas presents every year. He didn't get along with your father and that was another reason he left. Your father was a difficult man,' Sally tells her son.

'And where the hell is he?'

'He's remarried and seemingly happy.'

'Is he happy because he doesn't have to see me?'

'No, like Ryan he found it hard dealing with our family life.'

'But I never hit him, did I?'

'No, but he didn't get along with all of us and it was best for everyone when he moved out.'

'Why doesn't he ever send me any presents? He knows when it's my birthday and he must know when Christmas comes along.'

'Yes he does. Some parents are not close to their children and unfortunately your father wasn't that nice to you or Ryan.'

'So my father was an arsehole?'

'No, he just found it hard being a father,' Sally looks over at me. That was a diplomatic answer. She's told me on a number of occasions that her ex-husband was a philandering prick.

'So please don't blame Ryan for everything. It didn't bother me when you attacked me more,' Sally adds.

I'm sure it did.

'Do all mothers get the shit beaten out of them?' Kieran asks.

'No, not all.'

Hopefully very few.

'So the next time we meet Ryan are you going to be nicer to him?' I ask.

'Only if he doesn't sell my presents on eBay.'

That's as good as an answer as we're going to get right now. He hasn't rejected a second meeting but it might take more similar conversations to get him on board. Were these home truths the first time Sally's been this honest to Kieran? I don't know but they needed to be said. I was surprised at the level of aggression that Kieran displayed tonight, I thought that there was going to be bumps in the road but there's obviously a lot of pent-up resentment that he had kept hidden for so long.

As soon as Kieran is settled in the home I will contact Ryan and find out if he wants to see his brother again.

CHAPTER TWENTY FIVE: RYAN

I finish off the wine in the restaurant, pay the bill and make my way to the nearest pub. I order my drink and take a seat the furthest away from the big TV screen which is showing an Arsenal game and being the local team the pub is very crowded with football supporters. After I sit down I wonder if I should just leave and go to another pub but I'm just too exhausted both physically and mentally to make the effort.

Despite my many conversations with Sienna I still didn't know what to expect about seeing Kieran again but I genuinely did not anticipate his strange and uptight attitude towards me. The only time he seemed happy was when he first entered the restaurant and saw all the diner's meals, after that brief moment the atmosphere descended rapidly.

As the crowd cheer an Arsenal goal my mobile bleeps, it's Sienna.

'Kieran's back at home. He's calm. Good night staff on duty. Fancy meeting up?'

'Would love to. At the Queen's Head on Caledonian Road. Do you know it?'

'Yes, I'll be there in ten. You're not drunk already?' She texts with a laughing emoji.

'No, just got here,' I reply with a thumbs up emoji.

Sure enough within ten minutes she arrives. Soon after her text I got her a glass of white wine and handed it to her as she approached me.

'That's what I call excellent customer service,' she says.

'And that's the first compliment I've received today,' I reply.

'How do you feel about what happened at the restaurant?' Sienna asks.

'I think you already know the answer to that. He obviously remembers me leaving, even quoting me the exact date. Although he's barely mentioned me throughput your time with him there's no doubt there's still bitterness towards me and I don't blame him. I should've been there to help Mum deal with him but I was young and immature and just left Mum to it without any guilt. He really seems to hate me. I thought he was going to hit me after I asked about his favourite chocolate. I was shocked at how angry he became after what was an innocent question. Even when he did give me a half decent reply he looked directly at Mum instead of me, which I found strange. It was all extremely unsettling and I don't know where to go from here.'

'I perfectly understand why you feel down because I do as well but on the way home Sally, Kieran and myself had an interesting discussion which was quite enlightening.'

'How so?'

'First of all Sally really talked you up saying that you never retaliated despite the intense provocation and she tried to justify why you left home.'

'Oh yeah, how did she explain that?'

'You found the family dynamic too stressful and wanted some breathing space. Then we got into the situation with your father. She again tried to justify his actions to Kieran without revealing much of the truth.'

'I'd love to meet up with that bastard again just to let him know how much I hate him. You'd think that at some point in his life he'd want to know how his two sons are doing but I suppose I'm the wrong person to judge him on that. All the same, I hope one day, before he's too decrepit to know what's going on, to let him know how badly he treated everyone in the family and how damaged we all are.'

'Kieran did say something that was extremely relevant. When you left he saved all his physical assaults that were meant for you and basically transferred them to Sally, so for a long period she was badly attacked. He tried to explain that he had to fulfil some target which he set himself everyday. That's what it sounded like anyway.'

'Wow, so my mother got my share of pinches and head butts on top of what she normally got?'

'Yep.'

'Just when I thought I couldn't feel much worse…'

'I have to be totally honest with you if we're going to progress with this. I'm surprised a lot of this stuff hasn't been brought up before but maybe it has,' Sienna says.

'So where do we go from here? Does he actually want to see me again?'

'Only if you don't sell his presents on eBay,' she replies smiling.

'Did he really say that?'

'Yeah, he seems to think that you kept his presents deliberately.'

'Well I do have an obsession for glass-cutting. Seriously though, here are his presents,' I hand over the carrier bag.

'What were your impressions of him? Did you recognise some of his behaviours from before?' Sienna asks me.

'When I lived with him his behaviours baffled me. No one else I knew had the same family issues. I didn't try to understand why he behaved the way he did, it just pissed me off. I know I'm repeating myself but I was too young to comprehend what was going on with him. If I had to compare the thirteen-year-old teenager that I left behind to the person I saw today it's like looking at two different people but both having very strange behaviours which I still don't understand. Maybe I need to study autism more and although I've been looking at a number of articles online recently there's nothing I've read that explains the behaviour I witnessed today. There's definitely an element of resentment there which would be the case even if he wasn't autistic but the manner in which it manifests itself is hard for me to comprehend if that makes any sense. For example his aggressive reaction to my chocolate question was bizarre. Can you explain that?' I ask Sienna.

'No, not entirely, you could've said just about anything and he would've jumped all over you. As you said earlier he never mentioned you when I was with him but he seems to remember everything and I didn't anticipate that. How do you feel about seeing him again? Has it put you off?'

'If I'm honest, it's something I'll have to think about. I hope once the dust settles I'll be in a better frame of mind to try again but can I sleep on that?'

'Of course, there's a lot to take in.'

'I'm pleased that my mother defended me. I have to admit I completely misjudged her for so many years. Yes, she totally blanked me from the moment when Kieran's problems started to emerge but I never saw it from her point of view. When I witnessed her calm reaction after Kieran spat in her face it just brought it home to me what an extremely difficult life she's had, with no help whatsoever. I've wasted too many years feeling bitter towards her and I regret that as I've got older. I couldn't see it from her perspective. I'll ring her later to see if she wants to meet up tomorrow morning, I'd like to have another chat with her. I'm sure she's not feeling great right now.'

I take a sip of my beer.

'Will we ever spend any time together when we're not talking about Kieran?' I ask.

'Isn't that the whole reason we're here?'

'Yes, but wouldn't it be nice if we could spend an evening just chin-wagging about bullshit?'

'Didn't we do that last week when you kept banging on about *It's A Wonderful Life*?' She replies, smiling.

'I challenge you not to shed a tear or two at the end of that film.'

'You're on, what's the wager?'

'A day trip to Brighton. The loser pays the train fare and lunch.'

'Wow, you must be confident you'll win.'

'I am, but don't look up the ending beforehand otherwise the bet is void.'

'OK, so when is this film premiere going to happen?'

'Whenever you want. I'll cook the dinner. What do you fancy?'

'That lasagne you made a couple of weeks ago was just superb. I wouldn't mind having that again. A Saturday or a Sunday are the best days for me.'

'How about five o'clock this Saturday at mine?'

'It's a date... well not actually a date but you know what I mean.'

'Yeah, I do.'

We spend a very pleasant couple of hours unwinding after what was an emotional and stressful experience at the restaurant. Whether Sienna cries or not at the end of *It's A Wonderful Life*, it looks like we're going to spend a day at Brighton. I'm so excited at that prospect but first I've got to meet my mother to get her thoughts about our restaurant meeting with Kieran before the date that's not a date.

CHAPTER TWENTY SIX:
SIENNA

'Do you know if there's any rules about dating a sibling of a resident?' I ask Mandy.

'I'm not sure, I presume you're referring to that rather good looking guy, Ryan?'

'Yes,' I sheepishly reply.

'Has anything happened yet?' Mandy asks, smiling.

'No, but I'm beginning to have feelings for him and I think he likes me too but if it's against the rules I don't want to lose my job.'

'Is there a conflict of interests? I don't think so but you'd have to speak to HR about that. Anyway how did it go yesterday with Kieran and Ryan?'

'Not good but I'm hoping we'll get another chance. Mandy, sorry to rush off but I've got to see Kieran, I'll fill you in later.'

There are no structured course lessons in our 'home' but we do have Art, IT and life skills classes. We also take the residents on outings for part of the week, which includes swimming, trampolining (a particular favourite and burns off energy), visits to shops, towns, the cinema, theatre etc. If it's feasible the residents sometimes choose the day's activities.

Friday is my one to one day with Kieran.

'I've got a couple ideas about what we can do today. As it's a lovely morning why don't we go walking in Finsbury Park?' I ask Kieran.

'Impossible, it's bad luck to walk on grass on a Friday.'

That's news to me.

'You like art, why don't we go the National Gallery?'

'Nah, all the artists in that building are dead so what's the point?'

'What about the cinema, there's that new Batman film?'

'No, Batman doesn't laugh anymore, he's too serious but at least he admits he can't fly.'

I presume this is a reference to the Peter Pan debacle a couple of weeks ago.

I then remembered that on my way home last night I saw a poster advertising a Bob Denny work in progress gig today in Piccadilly Circus. I got up later than usual this morning and rushed to get here on time so it completely slipped my mind until now.

'Just wait here, I've got to make a quick phone call,' I tell Kieran.

'Alright but make it quick cos I've got things to do today.'

I thought that's what we were just discussing.

As soon as I leave the room I ring the theatre.

'Hello, are there any tickets left for the Bob Denny gig today?' I ask.

'Yes, plenty.'

'Can I buy two please?'

'I can get you two tickets on the front row.'

This is always a dilemma when booking seats near the stage for a comic gig. Is it too close for comfort?

But I just know that Kieran would be thrilled to be so near his idol.

'OK, that's fine but is there any possibility that this gig will be cancelled? The reason I'm asking you this is because we were booked to attend one of his gigs a few weeks ago but it was cancelled hours before the performance and I was going with an autistic adult and he got extremely upset. I'm going with that same person today and I just want to make sure that it's all going ahead.'

'Between you and me the ticket sales have been poor and I've been told that it will definitely go ahead. A couple of BBC executives are coming down this afternoon as they're making a documentary on old comics who have maybe peaked in their career.'

You mean has-beens?

'That's wonderful news. Thanks.'

'If you give me your email address I'll send the tickets to you. Well I hope you and the BBC chaps enjoy the show.'

Having secured the tickets I return to Kieran.

'What took you so long? I hate waiting.'

I can confirm that.

'How about going into Piccadilly Circus? We can walk around the theatres and maybe get a bite to eat.'

'Will Anthony Hopkins be there?'

'No, I don't think so.'

'I won't go then. I loved that film where he eats humans. I wonder if he puts any ketchup on their bodies before eating them? Does he have humans for breakfast instead of Corn Flakes?'

'I'm pretty sure he doesn't eat humans for breakfast, but there's plenty other actors in the West End plays.

Maybe we can try and get a selfie or an autograph if we can find an actor that you like.'

'Who's going to be there?'

I pick up a *TimeOut* magazine and study the theatre section.

'David Mitchell's in a play. You liked him in *Peep Show*.'

'What play is it?'

'It's a comedy about Shakespeare.'

'Shakespeare? Isn't he that writer bloke?'

'Yeah, he wrote a few plays that were rather popular.'

'But he's dead isn't he?'

'Yes, Shakespeare's no longer with us.'

'Not interested in laughing at dead people.'

'OK, the Strictly Come Dancing live show is on. You like that and could get plenty of selfies there.'

'I only like them dancing in the TV studios, if they're dancing in the street outside the theatre then I don't want anything to with them.'

'I don't think they'll be dancing outside the theatre.'

'I can't take that risk. They all have dancing OCD - every time I see them they can't stop dancing. They're obsessed with it.'

Once again his logic baffles me. I'm attempting to use any excuse to get him to Piccadilly Circus as I don't want to tell him the real reason we're going there in case of a cancellation. I know that the theatre lady was pretty convinced that this wasn't going to happen but I'll wait until a few minutes before the show is about to begin before telling him. I left my mobile number with the theatre so if I don't get a call or an email from them I'll assume it's all OK. I don't want to get beaten up again. I am pleased that the performance is in the afternoon because that frees up time afterwards to either get a bite to eat or more celebrity stalking.

'I've found a good one - Kelsey Grammer. He's in a play. You love Frasier.'

'What's the play about?'

'A man struggling with his life after his divorce.'

'What a load of old bollocks. Is he playing Frasier in it?'

'No, it's nothing to do with Frasier but if we wait by the stage door we might get a selfie with Frasier… I mean Kelsey.'

He shakes his head. I can tell from his facial expression that he's losing interest in my celebrity stalking approach so I need to come at it from a different angle.

'They have Burger King in Piccadilly Circus,' I say.

'OK, count me in.'

So Burger King succeeded where Shakespeare, Frasier and some OCD dancers failed.

At lunchtime we travel on the London Underground to Piccadilly Circus and head straight to Burger King. As Kieran tucks into his Big Whopper and fries I'm constantly checking my phone for any theatre cancellation emails or messages but so far nothing. I feel extremely tense as I desperately want to pull this off.

Kieran, like most of the StarLight residents, is obsessed with food. I suppose they don't have too much in their life, so if it brings them some pleasure by occasionally indulging them with a fast food meal then it's all worth it and Kieran is definitely in a better frame of mind after his meal.

At exactly two-twenty-five we reach the theatre and Kieran's eyes nearly pop out of his head when he sees the Bob Denny poster.

'Are you teasing me again?' He asks me.

'What do you mean?'

'Pretending to go to a Bob Denny show and then making some excuse why we can't go.'

'Not that this ever happened but no, this is for real. Now come on, the show starts in a few minutes.'

The look of pure joy on his face is priceless. We take our front row seat seconds before the lights go down. It's an extremely small theatre, at a guess I'd say a two hundred capacity but there are only a few audience members here. That must be soul destroying for Denny.

When Denny enters the stage to a smattering of audience Kieran gives his hero a standing ovation before he utters a word. I thought that this adored reaction was exclusively reserved for musical icons such as Sinatra, Presley, Lennon, McCartney, Dylan and the like. Well it looks like Denny has joined that elite club.

'Thank you, sir and what is your name?' Denny asks Kieran.

'I'm Kieran Doyle. I was born on the eighteenth of May 1996 and I love grass. You were born on the seventh of June 1957. You had your own TV series from 1986 to 1991 and you've played the London Palladium five times. What confuses me is that you've never been honoured by the Queen or the King for your amazing career. You're the best comedian on the planet earth'

'Wow, a simple 'Kieran' would've sufficed.'

A few people laugh at this but Kieran just stares at Denny.

'You can sit down now, Kieran, but thanks for that lovely welcome. That reminds me, each time I played the Palladium it was always a sell out. If memory serves me correctly the capacity there is 2,286, now let me count how many people are here tonight… one, two, three…'

An embarrassing silence fills the theatre.

'Nineteen, wow that says it all about my career. Still I'm here to entertain all of you and that's what I will try to do.'

At that moment a couple walk out the theatre.

'Make that seventeen.'

'My fiancée and I were talking about life after we get married and she said she'd like to have children one day. I told her that was fine, but no longer than that.'

Kieran is the only person to laugh.

Denny again looks down at Kieran.

'I'm glad you came tonight. I've met you before haven't I?'

'Yes, on October 26th 2019. That was the best night of my life.'

'You truly are a massive fan. Would you like to sing a song with me?'

Kieran suddenly starts crying. I put my arm around him to comfort him but Denny jumps down from the stage and hugs him.

'Let's do it, Kieran,' he says, pointing to his musician on the piano who immediately starts playing *Sweet Caroline*. I'm standing right next to Kieran and Denny and start recording their duet on my iPhone. Kieran knows every line of this song as Denny sings it at all of his gigs and unbelievably their voices blend well and they get a much louder round of applause when the song ends. There is no doubt Denny noticed his 'I have AUTISM please be patient' lanyard so to include him in a duet again speaks volumes for him. Kieran's exuberant facial expression when the song ended brings me to tears. I just wish Ryan was here to witness this but at least I have the video to show him.

'I need you by my side to re-vitalise my career,' he tells Kieran. He then launches into his next joke.

'I said to my wife 'I have taught our dog Morse code. Then the dog tapped his paw... My wife asked 'what did he say?' 'Woof' I replied.

This time most of the audience laugh at this joke which seems to energise Denny as he continues to deliver jokes that get a positive audience reaction. This is the first time I've seen Denny live although I've sat through many of his DVDs with Kieran and to my surprise (and maybe even shock) I've been impressed at just how good he is. I suppose these guys have been doing this for so long they must have a good idea about what works. Maybe his lack of television appearances in the last couple of decades could be contributed to the fact that he is probably considered old fashioned and out of touch, especially with the emergence of alternative comedy back in the Eighties. As it's a work in progress set, his performance lasts only forty-five minutes and at the end he gets a rousing (ish) reception. After the excruciating opening he rallied and delivered a very solid and funny performance. As soon as it ends we both dash to the stage door, as this time we are definitely not going to miss the opportunity of a selfie or autograph.

A few minutes later Denny appears at the stage door. He's talking to a couple of guys, both of whom are wearing expensive looking suits. I'm assuming these are the BBC chaps.

'Ah, here's the man in question,' Denny says pointing to Kieran.

'Can I get a photo with you?' Kieran asks as he looks in awe at Denny.

'Of course but first let me introduce you to these guys...'

'Not interested, they look like arseholes.'

Denny and the BBC guys laugh but Kieran's stern expression remains. I'm guessing he's a bit pissed off because these guys are stopping him from getting that much sought after photo.

'Let me tell you something, Kieran, I'm not sure if you were aware but the BBC filmed the gig tonight and they loved it, that's what they told me anyway. And I've got you to thank for that. When I walked on stage and saw only nineteen people and that included these two,' Denny says, pointing to the BBC executives, 'I was ready to walk off stage there and then and that would've possibly put pay to my faltering career but your heartfelt response touched me and galvanised me into putting in a strong performance.'

'Can I get a photo?' Kieran replies.

'You haven't listened to a word I've said, have you?' Denny replies, smiling.

I take several photos of them both and Kieran's facial expression is a dream. Denny goes back into the theatre and collects several signed photos, books and DVDs and hands them all to Kieran.

One of the BBC guys approaches me.

'We're definitely going to use the footage of Kieran talking to Bob at the beginning and also when he booed him a couple of times for the jokes he didn't like, so do you mind signing these consent forms for us to use the footage. I'm assuming you're his carer?'

'Of course, no problem. I'll get Kieran to counter sign it. And let me apologise on his behalf for calling you arseholes.'

He laughs. 'No need to apologise. I like the fact that he just says what he's thinking.'

'Yes, but it does get him into trouble sometimes.'

'I'm sure it does. I just know the viewers are going to love this section of the documentary and I think it's going to do an awful lot of good for Bob's career.'

'How many comedians are in this documentary?'

'Eight, and the viewers will vote for the top three comics and they will then get to play the London Palladium. Bob stands an excellent chance of getting there. If you leave me your email address I'll let you know when the documentary is being shown.'

'The twenty-second joke about the window cleaner losing his rag was utter shit and the one about the new social media app for Bugs Bunny called WhatsApp Doc was just silly, so are you going to remove them from your act, because if you love your audience you should never tell those jokes again.'

'I did pick up on the fact you didn't like them when you started booing me and I'm going to take your valued advice and not include them anymore.'

We chat with Denny and the BBC executives for a bit longer before heading home.

Before we reach StarLight, Kieran replayed his video half a dozen times, in addition to just staring at the many photos I took of them both. He is without doubt the happiest I've ever seen him and I suppose that's only natural when you've just met the person you admire the most 'on the planet earth.'

As soon as he gets back to StarLight he shows all the other residents and care workers his Denny video and goodies and they are all thrilled for him.

I wonder if I'm now forgiven for the Wimbledon cancellation. Somehow I doubt it. But I am truly delighted for him. As I said earlier, these autistic adults live a very restricted life where simple daily tasks that we all take for granted sometimes seem insurmountable for many of them, so to experience a joyous moment is just wonderful to witness.

I'm not sure if Kieran will get much sleep tonight but my day is done. Just before I leave StarLight I send Ryan and Sally the Kieran/Denny video and in Ryan's text I type 'it really is a wonderful life.'

CHAPTER TWENTY SEVEN: RYAN

Yesterday I met my mother for coffee. She still seemed a little down after the eventful reunion but did strongly encourage me to try again. She told me that she was heading back to Blackburn as she thought it would make things less complicated should there be a second meeting. She said the fact that Kieran kept replying to her rather than myself whenever I asked him a question just re-enforces her decision and I agree with her. However it will expose me more as Sienna and Mum shield me from my brother.

We chatted for a couple of hours. She filled me in on more events that happened, good or bad, in Kieran's life after I left. I apologised again for misjudging her so harshly and not contacting her for so many years but she in turn apologised for all the parental mistakes she made with me. It was a morning of apologies.

But last night her mood was much lighter after we both received the wonderful Kieran and Bob Denny video. She was thrilled for her son because she knew how much it meant to him. Until Sienna told me about Kieran's obsession with the comic I thought that Bob Denny was dead.

My mood today has also picked up. This can be attributed to seeing that video coupled with the fact that very shortly Sienna will be arriving for the film night.

As per her request I have made lasagne, with meatballs, pasta and salad. There is also a bottle of red wine to accompany the dinner. There have been so many times in the past couple of weeks when I have longed to kiss her and ask her out for a date but it's complicated because of her professional relationship with my brother. I wonder if she feels the same. The sound of the doorbell interrupts my thoughts.

'On time as always,' I say as I give her a hug.

'My parents were a little OCD about timekeeping, I guess I've inherited that from them.'

She hands me a bottle of wine.

'The dinner's ready if you want to eat now?'

'OK, why not?'

She looks absolutely stunning, wearing a very short sky blue skirt, matched with the same colour top that looks a size too small; not that I'm complaining.

'I know that this is a film night but I just wanted to ask you your thoughts on seeing your brother again,' she says as I start dishing out the dinner.

'How long have you been here?' I reply.

'What do you mean?'

'How long have you been inside my flat?'

'A couple of minutes.'

'And you're already pressurising me about Kieran. Let me have at least a couple of glasses of wine before we start on that subject matter.'

'I'm sorry, I didn't mean to…'

'I'm only kidding.'

She looks at me with a bemused expression.

'I gave it a lot of thought and I'd like to give it another go. What did you have in mind?'

'As Sally has opted out of this one I initially thought that you and Kieran should do something on your own.'

'You're kidding me, right?'

'Hold on. I decided against it mainly for road safety reasons.'

'That's a relief.'

'Are you scared of him?' She asks me.

'Yes, in a way I am. He's totally unpredictable in what he says and does and that's unnerving. Plus I don't think he likes me.'

'I know he was aggressive with you and that won't disappear overnight. He's usually like that when he meets new people and because of the background between you both it's just heightened.'

'OK, where do you suggest we go?'

'A walk in the park? Supermarket shopping?. A pub visit or just going for a coffee? You need to spend time with him.'

'OK, let's keep it simple - how about a walk in Finsbury Park?' I propose.

'Sounds perfect. Are you available tomorrow?' She asks.

'Yes but will he agree to it?'

'I'm pretty confident he'll be up for it. He's been in such a good mood since the Bob Denny gig so it's as good a time as any to ask him. I'll let you know first thing tomorrow morning.'

'Did you hand him back the presents?'

'Yes I did. He seemed a little surprised as he was convinced you were going to sell them or keep them for yourself.'

'You see, that's what I mean about trying to get inside his head. Why would he think like that?'

'I'm afraid I don't know all the answers, autism is a minefield.'

'OK, from now on it's going to be a Kieran free evening, agreed?' I say as I raise my wine glass.

'Agreed.'

We click glasses.

'What sort of trouble did you get into after you left home? You never told me.' Sienna asks as we start our meal.

'The flat I was renting was in a pretty rough housing estate and after a while I befriended some of the guys there, most of whom didn't have too much respect for the law. You've got to remember that I was young and very angry so I soon fell into a routine of nicking stuff from various local shops. If I needed some tools I would simply go into the local DIY shop and take them without paying. I must've done it about a dozen times before I was caught.'

'And what happened then?'

'I got thirty hours community service, cleaning the streets, old people's gardens, that type of thing.'

'Did it deter you?'

'No, not the first time. I continued nicking stuff but when I got caught again the judge gave me fifty hours community service and warned me that if it happened again it would be a prison sentence and that really scared me, so that was the end of my criminal lifestyle.'

'Did you work on your own or part of a gang?'

'A bit of both and nearly all the guys who were with me eventually ended up in prison so I was lucky I got out when I did. I hope they mended their ways because nearly all of them came from broken homes and left school at the first opportunity. They really had nothing to look forward to other than the thrill of stealing and getting away with it.'

'Did you ever take drugs during that time?'

'No never, although some of the others did, mainly cocaine.'

'Are you still in contact with any of them?'

'No, I moved out of there after a year and then went to college for my plumbing certifications.'

'Did you blame Kieran and Sally for your criminal indiscretions?'

'Are you sure you didn't apply for Jeremy Paxman's job when he left *NewsNight*?'

'Very funny.'

'Yes I did blame them for the mess I was in. Because of my awful family life I had to leave home and ended up in a shitty flat in a shitty area as I couldn't afford anything else. As you know that bitterness stayed with me for a very long time. Anyway I thought we weren't going to talk about all of that tonight.'

'Yeah, sorry.'

'Since we've met you've been asking me question after question but I still don't know too much about you other than your parents are divorced and you recently split up with some guy called Philip so why don't you tell me a bit more about yourself?'

'Not much to tell really. Compared to your upbringing it's been pretty uneventful. Overall I had a happy childhood but I do remember being really stressed out when my parents split up. I was only thirteen at the time. Mum's affair ended their marriage, it's as simple as that. I went to university and passed all my exams but didn't know what type of career I wanted. I saw a TV programme about autism and it really struck a chord with me. My parents thought that I could've got a better job with a bigger salary but once they could see how passionate I was about my work they relented. I've had a few boyfriends but nothing that lasted more than a few months. Philip was my longest relationship. Anyway that's about it.'

'Do your parents get along?'

'Yes, mostly, but they don't see much of each other. I spent Christmas Day with Dad and Boxing Day with Mum, next Christmas it'll be the reverse. They're both good people, I don't have too many issues with them.'

'Did they like Philip?'

'I think they tolerated him. Whenever I discussed Philip with my father I could tell that he wasn't bowled over by him but he never slagged him off, however on one occasion after a couple of Guinness's he did let his guard down and told me that Philip had 'airs above his station'. I actually laughed when he said that because I knew it was true.'

'Thanks for sharing that although I do think there's more to be told.'

'Believe me there isn't.'

We finish the meal and settle down to watch *It's A Wonderful Life*. As usual I'm sitting in the armchair and Sienna has the couch.

After explaining the background to a couple scenes in the film she explains 'I get the plot, I'm not a simpleton.'

After the sentimental film ending I glance over at Sienna who grabs a tissue and wipes her eyes.

'Got something in your eye?' I ask.

'OK, you win the bet.'

'I knew it, I knew it. That ending still gets to me and I've seen it a million times. Brighton here we come. Do you know any five star Michelin restaurants there?'

'Not sure about that but I know they have an excellent McDonalds right opposite the pier. I have to admit I thought that was an amazing film and I'm baffled why I haven't seen it before. Thanks for sharing it with me and of course for the superb meal.'

'You're not leaving already? Have another glass.'

'OK, one more but I've had a busy week and it's beginning to catch up on me right now.'

'You can always sleep over, I'll kip on the sofa.'

There's an awkward silence before she responds.

'Thanks but I'm only a few tube stops away.'

I offer to get Sienna an Uber but she declined. I then asked if she wanted me to accompany her to the tube station but she told me that wasn't necessary. We embrace each other but she pulls away quickly. I wonder if I was too forward in asking her to stay. Did she think there was an ulterior motive? So a wonderful evening ends on a subdued note. Maybe our relationship will remain a friendly but professional one.

CHAPTER TWENTY EIGHT: SIENNA

I arrive at work on time as usual but I've hardly slept at all. I kept thinking about my night with Ryan. Should I have accepted his offer to stay the night? But I don't want to take our relationship to another level until I'm sure that personally and professionally it's the right move. I did email head office yesterday for clarification on the company rules about dating a resident's sibling without mentioning my personal circumstances but all I got was an automated 'we're dealing with your inquiry' reply.

I think Ryan's invitation was an innocent and considerate gesture so maybe I'm reading too much into this.

The normal office hours of nine to five, Monday to Friday just don't apply to my job. I have to work at least two Sundays out of four. This used to really piss off Philip as he was always arranging social events at weekends. On many occasions I would turn up at some highfalutin event in my work clothes as I didn't have time to change. I can still picture his disappointment when he noticed my attire, seemingly embarrassed, as he was usually surrounded by all his rich friends.

But today I've got to speak to Kieran about Ryan and there's no time like the present.

He's in his bedroom watching 'surprise, surprise' one of the DVDs Bob Denny gave to him. This bodes well as there's a reasonable chance that he's in a good mood.

'How's the video?' I ask.

'Absolutely astonishing. He cracks me up every time he opens his mouth. The only thing I don't like is his hair. No hair in the middle but loads of it on the sides. I wonder if he should cut the sides and glue them to the top of his head and then I'll be able to see his ears.'

I always have a chuckle to myself when I see a man wearing a wig because nine times out of ten the wig looks like it came free with a packet of Corn Flakes. So in fairness I don't think Denny's got anything to lose by implementing Kieran's hair suggestion.

'Kieran, how do you feel about going for walk in Finsbury Park with me and Ryan?'

'I'm not sure he likes grass.'

'Yes he does and he wants to see you again.'

'Why?'

'Because he's your brother and he wants to get to know you better.'

'He's got a few grey hairs on his head, I don't like that.'

It's that hair obsession again.

'That just comes with getting a bit older. It happens to most people. It's nothing to worry about.'

'I don't want to look at his grey hairs again but I'll go to the park with you.'

'OK, what if I tell him to dye it, would that be acceptable?' I ask the hair specialist.

'Yeah, dye it black just like Naga's,' he replies.

'His hair's brown it's probably best if he uses a brown dye.'

'Nah, Naga has black hair and she's always smiling unless she's talking to some arsehole politician who is talking as if they've just climbed out of a rubbish bin.'

That's a little abstract but nevertheless a valid point.

'Also his hair's too long so he needs to get it cut short. Doesn't he know that he'll grow deaf if his hair is covering his ears?'

I suspect that medical observation is not accurate but Kieran is the expert on unusual facts so I'm not ruling it out just yet.

'So you're saying that if Ryan cuts his hair short and dyes it black then you'll meet him in the park?'

'Correct, now if you don't mind clearing off, I need to watch the emperor of comedy.'

For some reason I really felt confident that there wouldn't be an issue getting the brothers together this time around but now I've got to speak to Ryan to find out if he will agree to Kieran's demands.

This will test how much he wants to see his brother again.

I ring his mobile.

'Hi ya, what's up?' He asks.

'How much do you like your hair?'

'What do you mean?'

'If I ask you to get a number one buzz and dye it black this morning would that be OK?'

'After first questioning your sanity my next response would be a negative one. What's all this about?'

I explain Kieran's terms and conditions.

'He must be winding you up,' Ryan responds.

'That's really not in his nature and not typically an autistic trait. He's serious and if you want to see him again you'll have to do it. Your hair will grow back, well most of it anyway, and it really won't be long before your grey hairs reappear.'

'So you've noticed my bald spot then?'

'Only when you bent down to tie up your shoelaces.'

'Is nothing sacred?'

Even though he can't see me I smile back at him.

'Does that mean I'll have to keep shaving my hair and stock up on hair dye for the rest of my life?'

'Let's deal with one thing at a time. It's your call but personally I think you'll regret it if you back out.'

'I've always had my hair long.'

'It's a small price to pay. Sooner or later you could well end up looking like Bob Denny so it's a good opportunity to cut it short, to minimise the bald spot.'

'Wow, you really cut to the chase.'

'Sorry if that sounded harsh, that's not what I intended.'

There's silence at the other end of the line. He's obviously mulling it all over.

'I hate putting you on the spot but we're going to the park this afternoon and I need to know if you're going to be joining us.'

'A dog with ... OK, I'll go to the barbers right now.'

'Good, I'll await your phone call and by the way just tell Kieran that you love grass.'

'Thanks for the surreal conversation. I'll be in touch,' with that he hangs up.

I think he's beginning to learn that the rules and values in the autistic bubble are dissimilar to the rest of society. Although he grew up with an autistic brother, the thirteen-year-old boy he left behind all those years ago is very different from the man today.

I seek out Kieran.

'Your brother's going to dye his hair and get a haircut. Are you happy about that?' I ask him.

'What time is this happening?'

'He's going to the barbers right now.' Let's hope that none of his customers have burst pipes or boilers not working on this chilly morning.

'Has he got an appointment?'

'No, he's just going to turn up.'

'What happens if there're fully booked? I can't wait around all day, I need to get going,' Kieran responds, looking at the dining room clock.

Most of the residents are very driven by the clock, almost as if every minute of the day cannot be wasted, when in reality they have all the time in the world.

I think I was too blunt with my comments concerning Ryan's hair, especially likening him to Denny. I can't imagine anyone being pleased with that comparison. But in my defence I wanted to make the point that if he really wanted to develop a relationship with his brother, then getting a hair cut isn't such a big deal. However, it must have come as a bit of a shock so maybe I should have approached it more delicately.

I've laid awake at night many times recently questioning whether I've done the right thing in pursuing this reunion. I seem to spend more time dealing with this rather than concentrating on my day job. It's taken its toll on me as I'm constantly pondering all the many scenarios but just when I come to the conclusion that I've bitten off more than I can chew, the fact that Ryan now has some sort of a relationship with Sally gives me a level of encouragement that I'm doing the right thing. However getting the brothers together has been an extremely stressful experience for all involved. I just hope that if they can meet up this afternoon in the wide open spaces of Finsbury Park, with little distractions, then I'll have a much better idea on whether it will work.

CHAPTER TWENTY NINE:
RYAN

It's amazing how quickly it took to become a baldie.
The buzzer takes no prisoners.

I stop off at Primark to purchase a woolly hat to
protect my hairless head against the cold weather. I'm
not quite at the Harry Hill stage just yet but not far off
it. This is the shortest I have ever had it and although I
look like a dickhead it's all for a good cause, or so I
keep telling myself.

Matteo, my normal hairdresser, didn't question why
I suddenly wanted this drastic change. I suppose they
have to deal with many varied requests on a daily basis.

I ring Sienna.

'Job done. So where and when do you want to meet
up?' I ask her.

'Congratulations for going through with it.'

'What choice did I have? Anything to avoid the Bob
Denny look.'

'I'm sorry if I was too harsh earlier.'

'No need to apologise. I'm just desperate to meet my
brother again, so where's it to be?'

'Do you know the main entrance to Finsbury Park,
where the Hope and Anchor pub is?'

'Yep, I've frequented that pub many times.'

'See you there in half an hour.'

'OK.'

'How do you feel about seeing Kieran again?'

'Anxious, but the hair cut has been a distraction. Let's hope it has the desired effect.'

'Me too. I'll see you soon.'

I agree with Sienna on the choice of venue. Kieran's mood at the restaurant on our last ill-fated gathering was driven by food. He thought that his meal should have been waiting for him as soon as he arrived but in reality he still got it pretty quickly, thanks to Sienna's intervention. The walk in the park should be much calmer, with less distractions. It will hopefully give us a chance to have a lengthy chat and get along better but I'm under no illusions that it's going to be a smooth ride.

I nervously approach the entrance to the park. I can see both Kieran and Sienna. Kieran is shuffling his feet from side to side which probably means he's either equally anxious or just impatient.

'What fucking time do you call this?' He shouts at me. I'm guessing it's the latter.

I look at my watch. 'It's one minute past two, sorry if I'm sixty seconds late,' I reply, a little irritated.

'Two o'clock was the time, where the hell were you?'

'OK, Kieran, it's not a problem. Ryan's had a busy morning. He's just come from the barbers,' Sienna says.

Kieran asks me to bend over so he can inspect the top of my head. He then slowly walks around me, staring at my non-existent hair.

'Your hair is now symmetrical and your ears are slightly bigger than they were in 2009 but there are still hairs in them so you need to go back to the barbers to sort that out.'

'Yeah, I'll do that,' I reply.

'You're lying, so I'll have to accompany you.'

'That's not necessary.'

'Yes it is. Can you ring the barbers now? And put it on loud speaker because I don't want you pretending you're speaking to the barbers when you're actually chatting to your dentist.'

I look at Sienna who nods so I do what I'm told.

'I'd like to make another hair appointment for tomorrow?' I ask Matteo.

'Ryan, you've got no hair left. Is this a wind up?' He replies.

'Stop bullshitting and get rid of his ear hairs,' Kieran shouts at the phone.

'I'm sorry, who's this?' Matteo asks.

'That's Kieran, he's my brother. Can I come in anytime tomorrow?'

'Yeah of course. I'm here all day but I don't remember any excessive hairs in your ears.'

'Are you cross-eyed?' Kieran adds.

'My brother's autistic,' I explain.

'OK, maybe I missed it. I'll see you tomorrow,' Matteo diplomatically responds.

Despite being a regular customer at the hairdressers I never mentioned Kieran to Matteo. Why would I get that personal about someone that I blocked out for a huge chunk of my life? I could tell that Matteo was a little startled with Kieran's spirited contributions to our conversation. After my time with Kieran today I'll make a quick pit stop at the hairdressers to give Matteo the heads up on Kieran so that he's as prepared as he ever can be for my ear/hair appointment tomorrow.

'Shall we go for a walk?' Sienna suggests.

Kieran walks at pace and we follow.

'Don't lose hope,' Sienna whispers to me.

I nod.

'You'll get used to his ways, I promise.'

'He's far more complicated than I remember. I'm scared to talk to him because whatever I say he's going to respond with a cutting remark. It seems to me that he's not going to forgive me for what I did and I can't blame him. I don't see a positive outcome to this.'

I'm speaking quietly even though Kieran is walking about a hundred feet ahead of us.

'I mean why get so angry about some non-existent hairs in my ears? I don't get it.'

'You know he has a hair obsession, hence your haircut. Try to engage with him and don't get too down with some of the things he says. I went through this same process when I first met him and now we get along just fine.'

'Didn't he beat you up recently?' I sarcastically ask.

'Although I don't minimise what he did it, was a one-off and I could've handled the situation better. Why don't you discuss Bob Denny with him? That's a relatively safe topic to start off a conversation.'

'OK, but I'm not sure there are any safe topics.'

'Just try.'

We catch up with Kieran.

'So how are you feeling today?' I ask my brother.

'Half and half.'

'Does that mean half good and half not so good?'

'I like walking on grass and I'm pleased that I can see your ears. It's so much better when your hair's not flopping everywhere in Finsbury Park.'

'OK, that's good but you're still anxious?'

'Yes.'

'About what?'

'You.'

'Why?'

'First of all you use way too much Sellotape. That's just too silly.'

'OK, I may have done that in the past and the reason I did that is because I wanted your presents to arrive safely. But in the last batch of presents I used no tape.'

'Yes and that confused me. Why did you change your Sellotape policy?'

'Sienna told me you were anxious about the Sellotape so I just gave you the presents without any wrapping.'

'I don't like it when people change their minds.'

As this conversation is going around in circles I decide to change tack.

'So are you going to see Mum soon?'

'Why do you call her mum?'

'Because she's my mother.'

'Is she? You didn't see my mother for loads of years so I thought that would disqualify you.'

'No, it never does. It's a lifelong relationship. Kieran, I'm sorry that I left you alone with my… your mother, but if I'm truthful I couldn't live in that house anymore. You rarely slept and were always hitting me; I just couldn't handle that. I should've stayed in contact and I'll never forgive myself for letting you and your mother down but I really want to make it up to you if you'll just give me a chance. I want to be your brother again.'

He approaches me with gritted teeth and promptly gives me a couple of hefty pinches in my upper arm.

'Fucking hell, Kieran, what did you do that for?' I shout at him.

He then gives me a kick in the shins which hurts like hell and causes me to fall onto the grass. Sienna steps across him to block any further attacks.

A middle-aged man walking his dog approaches me.

'Are you alright mate?' He asks.

'Yeah, no problem.'

'Do you want me to call the police?'

'No, he's my brother and he's autistic.'

The man looks at Kieran with a confused expression and slowly walks away.

'Kieran, you mustn't hurt Ryan, he was apologising to you, he did not deserve that assault,' Sienna says.

'But he never hits me back.'

'That's because he doesn't want to hurt you. He's never done that.'

Kieran looks down at me, his face still contorted with anger but turns around and starts walking away from us.

'I better go with him. Are you OK?' Sienna asks.

'Go ahead, I'll ring you later,' I reply.

Maybe I should have taken Sienna's advice to start off our conversation talking about Bob Denny but I wanted to explain to him why I left all those years ago.

The attack will no doubt leave some bruises on my arm and leg but in time they'll heal, however I'm not sure that my relationship with my brother will ever do the same.

CHAPTER THIRTY:
SIENNA

I was too angry to speak to Kieran for the rest of our walk in the park, not that he seemed that bothered as he also didn't utter a word. But this period of silence gave me time to reflect on what just happened.

It was six months after I started working with Kieran when I first discovered that he had a brother and even then I can count on one hand the number of times he's mentioned Ryan in conversation and only then in passing. However it's now obvious that Ryan's reappearance in his life has stirred up a lot of hidden resentment. The incident at the park confirmed Sally's initial fears that Kieran could revert to the aggressive behaviour that I saw on a daily basis in the first year of our working relationship. Whether he extends his hostile attitude to myself or other residents remains to be seen.

I felt bad leaving Ryan laying on the grass looking shell shocked after the physical assault. I have no idea what his thoughts are on pursuing his relationship with his brother but this attack must throw serious doubts on that ever happening. Has he got the physical and mental resolve to overcome this latest setback?

I'm also beginning to have my own misgivings. This reunion was instigated by me. It took a lot of persuasion to get Ryan and Sally on board so if it all goes pear shaped, I know where the buck stops.

Kieran is in the StarLight garden drinking a can of Sprite. I approach him.

'Do you want to talk about what happened in the park?' I ask him.

'I enjoyed it, there was no mud on my shoes.'

'Why did you attack your brother?' I ask, careful to hide my anger.

'He expects it.'

'No he definitely does not expect it. He told you earlier that one of the reasons he left home was because you kept hitting him so if you continue to do that he may decide not to see you again. Is that what you want?'

Kieran takes another sip of his Sprite.

'I feel calmer when I pinch someone. It puts me in a good mood.'

'Did you feel calm even when you saw your brother in pain, which was caused by you?'

He nods. 'It's up to him how he reacts, that's not my problem.'

'But you haven't done that for so long, why start again now?'

'I haven't had a good pinching experience since that Ryan bloke left our house on the Monday October the twelfth 2009. Doing it to Mum wasn't the same. Her arms are too small so it didn't relax me.'

'You've got to stop pinching him. How would you like it if someone kicked you in the shins?'

'I'd just buy a pair of football shin pads from Sports Direct. That'll work.'

'Do you want to see your brother again?'

'Only if he gives me a Mars Bar.'

'OK, I'll tell him that but I'm only going to arrange another meeting if you promise not to attack him again.'

'He turned up late and that pissed me off.'

'And is that why you hit him?'

'It put me in a bad mood,' Kieran replies without answering my question.

'He was only late by a minute.'

'He was still late which shows he doesn't give a toss about me.'

'That's incorrect. He loves you. Didn't he just crop off all his hair, and even dyed it, just because you asked him to?'

'Yes but he should be thanking me for that because now he can see everything much clearer without that mop of hair crashing into his eyes and plugging up his ears.'

I want to carry on with this discussion but it's best that I step away before I say something I'll regret.

Kieran made a very interesting point about feeling calmer after attacking Ryan. Part of my studies into autism included analysing the connection between autism and OCD. Autistic children/adults find the world a strange and bewildering place and a method of reducing this constant anxiety is to perform repetitive actions. In Kieran's case this is pinching and hitting other people, including himself. I know from observing the other residents that some of these behaviours come and go but nearly always return. In Kieran's case his pinching was constant throughout his childhood and continued until a couple of years ago when it gradually became manageable. I feel Kieran's behaviour is the result of his heightened anxiety caused by Ryan's return after so many years away.

So what do I do now? I need to speak to Ryan and Sally, but Ryan first.

I ring his mobile. He answers it on the second ring.

'Hello, how are you?' He asks.

'I'm fine but I was going to ask you the very same question.'

'Battered and bruised but I'll survive.'

'I didn't expect him to do that, I'm sorry.'

'You've got nothing to apologise for and I'm certainly not expecting a contrite phone call from Kieran any time soon. He's definitely picked up from where he left off. He's got a good memory.'

'I know it's a bit early to be asking you this, but are you going to want to see him again?'

'Do you really think I'm some sort of masochist? Why would I want to put myself through that again?'

'I perfectly understand where you're coming from…'

'But do you? You've no siblings so you can't possibly comprehend the intricacies of our family set up. OK, you know Kieran and are just amazing with him but being his sibling, albeit for only half of his life, is on another level and as you've just witnessed the feelings run very deep.'

'You're right but just because I don't have a brother of sister doesn't mean I don't understand what you're both going through and although Kieran is an extremely complex person I do have an idea what his trigger points are. I shouldn't have rang you so soon, emotions are running high. Give me a ring when you feel ready,' I say.

'Sienna, I didn't mean to be so abrupt, it's just…'

'No explanation needed. I'll give you time. Take it easy.'

I terminate the call before he has a chance to respond.

Because I didn't live through the same experiences as Ryan and Kieran I can't fully understand the depth of emotion the brothers feel but the fact I'm looking at it from the outside is not necessarily a bad thing. Unlike Kieran, who seems totally unaffected by the park encounter, Ryan's raw emotions are there for all to see. It doesn't sound like he wants to see Kieran again but I need to have that same conversation with him in a few days.

One down, one to go. I ring Sally.

'Is everything OK?' Sally asks, which is her go-to greeting. She's always expecting bad news and on this occasion she's going to get it.

'Ryan and Kieran just met up again. I didn't contact you beforehand as it was a last minute thing.'

'What happened?'

'For no obvious reason Kieran gave Ryan a few hefty pinches and kicked him in the shins.'

'Is Ryan OK?'

'Not really, he's very angry.'

'I'm going to ring him.'

'Sally, can you just leave it a day or two? You may find it even more upsetting if you talk to him now.'

'OK, but where do we go from here? It all goes back to my fear that Kieran will regress and that can't happen, even at the expense of not seeing his brother.'

'It was never going to be easy, we both knew that and today was definitely a setback. Kieran can't promise me that he won't hurt Ryan again so that leaves us in a very difficult position. Understandably Ryan's not keen to see his brother anytime soon. Personally, I think that once the dust settles it's worth another go but that is a discussion you've got to have with Ryan.'

'Lots to think about. I'll give Ryan some space to draw his own conclusions. Thanks for ringing,' Sally quietly responds before hanging up.

She cuts short our conversation which is unusual.

Is it too risky to arrange yet another meeting? Probably, but that decision is now out of my hands.

Just as I'm reflecting on the last two conversations, Jamie approaches me.

'Kieran tells me he beat the shit out of some bloke in the park. Was it because he said something rude about grass or Naga Munchetty?'

'The guy that Kieran pinched was his brother, Ryan and he didn't do or say anything wrong.'

'So why did he pinch him then?'

'I think he was in a bad mood because he thought Ryan turned up late.'

'Is that the new rule then? If I'm in a bad mood I can beat the crap out of everyone. I like that idea.'

'No, you must never do that. You'll get into trouble with the police.'

'But Kieran's in his bedroom laughing his head at Bob Denny's jokes and the old Bill obviously don't care, do they?'

'It's different because it was his brother.'

'Oh OK, the rule is if you're feeling a bit down you can beat the crap out of your brother and nobody else?'

'Don't physically hurt anyone under any circumstances is the rule.'

'These rules are so confusing,' he replies before leaving the room.

Teaching normal children is a stressful job but trying to teach the most basic concepts to autistic children and adults requires an awful lot of patience and guidance. However when the message is accepted and taken on board it is the most satisfying feeling ever and that's why I love my job so much. Even though all the residents are all in their mid to late twenties they have the innocence of a child which is so endearing but also makes them extremely vulnerable in the outside world.

Although the thought of having children myself has never been a realistic prospect up to now, I do feel incredibly protective of all the residents here. I will defend them against anyone, and I mean anyone, as any parent would.

The rest of the day was uneventful. I didn't discuss the park incident any further with Kieran as I just didn't have the energy.

I feel mentally and physically exhausted and leave work earlier than usual. The quietness in my home is welcoming and before I've even taken my coat off I plonk myself down on the sofa and pour a glass of wine. My thoughts are totally absorbed with what happened earlier. Despite telling Sally that we should give the brother reunion another try, for the first time I'm beginning to lose faith in Ryan and Kieran ever having a lasting relationship and that depresses me. I had moments today when I regretted ever prompting all of this but if nothing else it has brought Sally and Ryan together and that momentarily makes me feel better.

The main reason I started this process was because I felt with Sally's move to Blackburn it would leave Kieran more isolated than ever. It was done with good intentions but have I bitten off more than I can chew?

CHAPTER THIRTY ONE: RYAN

These past few weeks I have been extensively researching countless autistic topics on the internet but as yet I haven't looked at what triggers aggressive behaviours in autistic people so I google just that and it comes back with numerous links, ranging from medical and behavioural explanations to personal accounts from parents and care workers. There are articles on acute anxiety, sensory issues, breaks in routine, lack of sleep, communication difficulties, which includes understanding other people's needs and wants, facial expressions, body language etc. Apparently these personality traits can lead to aggressive tendencies. I notice with interest that there are a few articles about the effect this has on parents and care workers as they are often the victims of aggression.

I want to know if there is something that resonated with Kieran. Although a lot of these traits could apply to him I still think the root cause of his aggression right now is me.

My thoughts again return to yesterday's incident. I was too harsh with Sienna in our telephone conversation, she didn't deserve that. I'm sure she's equally distressed at how it all panned out. However for once her timing wasn't right when she asked if I wanted to see Kieran again only an hour after his attack on me. Although I was adamant that I didn't want to see my brother again, I'm still undecided. After reading those articles it brings it home to me again how difficult his life is. How can I ever understand his thought process? The world must be an extremely strange and confusing place to him and I have just added to that.

I'm sure my mother knows what happened yesterday and is probably equally distraught so I ring her.

'Hello, Ryan, how are you?' She quietly asks.

'I'm better. I presume Sienna told you what happened in the park?'

'Yes, and she suggested I give you a bit of space.'

'That was sweet of her. I was just a little shocked at the intensity of the attack. It's one thing when he did it to me as a child but quite another matter when struck by an adult but I should've expected it. He just doesn't like me and clearly doesn't want me in his life.'

'Ryan, he's so complicated. I can't even predict what he's going to do next but if you want to get to know him again you've got to persevere. Given my lack of parental guidance in the past I'm the last person to give you advice but to quote an old cliché, anything worth having is worth fighting for.'

'Hold on, it wasn't that long ago you were telling me to tread carefully as you were worried about Kieran reverting back to his old ways. What's changed?'

'I've been doing a lot of thinking since yesterday and although I'm still worried about him I do think it's worth the risk. You and me are all he's got.'

'And Sienna,' I say.

'Of course but she's not family.'

'I'm so torn...'

'I've a suggestion that'll help and I should've mentioned this before, whenever I meet Kieran I wear shoulder pads and shin pads. I can't remember the last time I wore a dress in his company. You'll still feel the hit but there's less impact.'

'I never thought about that.'

'It'll reduce your anxiety a little. It's not a game-changer but it helps.'

'That makes sense. I'll look into that straight away.'

'I just wish I'd thought about it earlier but I didn't know you were meeting Kieran yesterday.'

'Yeah, it was sort of sprung on me but your suggestion has given me renewed hope.'

'Does that mean you'll see him again?'

'I think so and this time I'll be more prepared, both mentally and physically.'

'You sound better already.'

'I feel better. I've got to make this work. I've got to make up for lost time.'

'So what are your plans?' My mother asks.

'The usual. Contact Sienna and try to arrange another get together. I was a little abrupt to her the last time we spoke so I owe her an apology.'

'I wouldn't worry too much about that. She's got a thick skin, she needs it as part of her job. Anyway you know that Kieran's starting his charity job tomorrow.'

'Yeah, I do. I hope it all goes well for him.'

'Me too. I better go, text me after you speak to Sienna and good luck. I'll be thinking of you.'

'Thanks, Mum. Are you coming down anytime soon?'

There's silence at the other end.

'Are you OK?' I ask.

'Yes, I'm fine. That's the first time you've called me Mum since you were a little boy.'

'Well you're beginning to feel like my mother now.'

'Better late than never. I won't come down just yet, I don't want to complicate things. Just take care.'

With that she hangs up.

I'm astonished at how well my relationship with my mother has developed. I never expected that to happen.

I now have to build up the same rapport with Kieran and although I know that's going to be much more difficult, I feel more optimistic since speaking to my mother. Her suggestion about wearing the shoulder and shin pads may be a way around the physical side of my relationship with my brother. All I have to do now is gain his trust.

CHAPTER THIRTY TWO:
SIENNA

'Do you have any Jeffery Archer books around the back?' A customer asks Kieran.

'Oh for fucks sake, I've lost my concentration now because of you. It took me twenty minutes to build up my concentration. Can you piss off?'

'I beg your pardon.'

'Did I interrupt you when you were looking for Archer?' Kieran says.

'I'm sorry, this is Kieran's first day. He's special needs,' I tell the customer.

She notices his 'I have AUTISM please be patient' badge and smiles faintly.

'I'll check and if I find one we won't charge you,' I say.

I manage to drag Kieran away from his DVDs to go to the back office. I'm afraid to leave him alone with this lady.

'Why were you so rude to that person? She was politely asking you a very simple question, if you don't know the answer just ask me or Miriam and we'll deal with it but please don't tell the customers to piss off.'

'But I was trying to sort the DVDs in alphabetical order before she interrupted me. I was up to Q so I'm going to have to start it all over again.'

'No, you don't have to start from the beginning, just pick it up from Q. Customers will be asking you questions throughout the day, we've talked about this. Just be polite to them, that's all.'

'If they interrupt my concentration again they'll get a kick up their arse.'

'Perhaps it's best if we work in the back office for now so no one will disturb you.'

'But I need to sort out the shop DVDs cos they're looking a mess. I was doing so well before that fat lady waddled in front of me.'

I have told him on numerous occasions to be more sensitive when describing a person's physical appearance but it obviously hasn't sunk it yet.

We manage to find Jeffery Archer's most famous book, *Kane and Able*. The lady was very grateful for the freebie – being told to piss off forgotten. Shortly afterwards Kieran returns to the shop floor to continue his DVD tasks, starting with titles beginning with the letter A. I never leave his side, fielding questions from the customers, keeping Kieran out of that loop.

'Oh look, they have a Michael McIntyre DVD, Jamie loves that man,' Kieran tells me.

'It's Jamie's birthday in a couple of weeks, why don't you buy it as a present for him?' I reply.

'But it's ninety-nine pence.'

'You can afford that.'

'Nah, that's too much, I'll give him one of the free gifts from my McDonalds meals.'

'But Jamie would be really pleased to get that DVD,' I say.

'McIntyre smiles too much, I don't want a smiling person in StarLight.'

It's that autistic thought process again.

Kieran gets on really well with Jamie but that friendship obviously doesn't extend to forking out ninety-nine pence for a present.

Sorting out DVDs is right up Kieran's street as ever since I've been involved with him he does this on a daily basis. He takes out his numerous DVDs and, depending on what day of the week it is, sorts them out by film title, leading actor/actress, director, producer, screenplay writer, main location of the film and the colour of the DVD cover. This is all part of his severe OCD.

The rest of the morning passes without incident. Although he didn't tell any more customers to piss off he did let an elderly chap know that his eyebrows were out of control and he should go and see a doctor about it. I admit his eyebrows were a little hairy but I don't think it required any NHS treatment. The man looked really confused when I apologised, saying that Kieran was autistic. I've seen that perplexed expression many times before because not everyone knows what autism actually is. That's hard to believe in this day and age but unfortunately it's true.

Upon leaving Full Of Heart Miriam hands Kieran two packets of chocolate digestives. He seemed really pleased to receive them but told Miriam 'the next time just give me some of those bank notes, I know for a fact that the bank has loads of them.'

That's another lesson on financial management that I've got to arrange.

Kieran's stint at Full Of Heart has definitely put him in a good mood. He seemed to take pride in the fact he did a good day's work and got rewarded for it.

During the ill-fated meeting in the park Kieran insisted that Ryan got his ear hairs trimmed. Although he did say he would accompany him to the barbers, luckily he hasn't followed up on that, however he has asked me several times if it's happened. Each time I have assured him it has but that hasn't stopped him asking again, almost as if he knows that I'm lying. As far as I know Ryan hasn't done this yet but he needs to before their next meeting otherwise it's all going to kick off again.

While Kieran relaxes in his bedroom I spend some time with Nicky. He's playing with his dry pasta, putting them into a plastic container one by one. He grunts as each one lands in the container. Mandy helps Nicky with this exercise every day. She is the primary carer for Nicky and I think she does an amazing job. Like Kieran, Nicky can get very aggressive and whilst I feel I can communicate with Kieran reasonably well I find it much harder trying to interact with Nicky as he is completely non-verbal. How the hell do you go through life without uttering one word and the frustration that must bring when he can't make himself understood to others? He does know some Makaton sign language but only on a basic level. Mandy thinks Nicky loves the sound that the dry pasta makes when it hits the plastic container.

After watching him perform this task for nearly an hour he puts the plastic container on the floor and stares at me. I know what's coming.

First of all he pinches the skin between my thumb and index finger. That may sound relatively minor but it hurts and he's gritting his teeth as he does it. He then pokes both my breasts. I hold his hands when he does this to minimise the impact but it still feels uncomfortable and inappropriate. He does this to Mandy several times every day. Like all the residents at StarLight, Nicky's behaviours are closely monitored by the staff and medical professionals and poking the breasts is not considered in any way sexual, it's just severe OCD behaviour and this action could be against any part of the body. Of course we discourage this behaviour and have used a number of strategies to combat it but it's a tough nut to crack. He did go through a phase of doing this to members of the public but luckily this was short-lived. Understandably this didn't go down well and resulted in a number of complaints even after explaining Nicky's disability.

He finishes off his daily routine by pinching my ears and stamping on my feet.

Nicky has limited interests, mainly food and music. Music has a calming influence on him. When he gets angry Mandy puts on an Ed Sheeran, U2 or Katherine Jenkins CD and eventually he relaxes by sitting next to the stereo. We recently went to a Simply Red concert and were sitting in the disabled section alongside the physically disabled people in their wheelchairs. We did get some strange looks as we took our seats as they must have thought we were just chancing our luck to get nearer the stage but they soon realised that disability comes in all shapes and sizes when Nicky wanted to topple over a couple of the wheelchairs with the guys in them. We were then situated a safe distance from everyone else.

After all the punching and poking Nicky rests his cheek against mine wanting a kiss and how can I refuse this lovely, innocent man? He then takes my thumb and index finger and shakes them up and down in an unconventional handshake.

In my opinion a lot of Nicky's aggression stems from not being understood. The Maketon signs that he uses are mainly when he's asking for food and telling us he's going to the toilet, anything more involved than that is extremely difficult for him. As Nicky is now twenty-nine and doesn't speak a word there is very little hope that he will ever speak. However he does have speech therapy lessons every week and one of the concepts used is something called receptive language skills which is the 'input' of language, the ability to understand and comprehend spoken language. Nicky does understand what I'm saying to him as long as it's a simple command. For example if I say 'can you fetch me your shoes from your bedroom' he always understands, even if he's not looking at me, but if I say something like 'what do you think of Jack Nicholson's performance in *One Flew Over The Cuckoo's Nest*?' He would just stare blankly at me.

Mandy enters the room.

'How's he been?' She asks.

'Just great. Isn't that right, Nicky?'

Nicky just continues with his dry pasta routine and ignores me. I don't take offence as this activity takes preference over everything.

'I'll take over now, Sienna. Thanks so much for giving me a break,' Mandy tells me.

I smile at her. This job is all consuming and takes its toll so it's nice to be able to help out a colleague. Mandy and the other carers here all do an amazing job. Because we all work different shifts we rarely get together socially which is a shame because we all get along so well and it would be nice to get more insight into their own lives.

Just as I'm leaving my phone rings, it's Ryan.

'Have you got a minute?' He asks.

'Of course, what's up?'

'First of all I want to apologise for the way I talked to you yesterday. I wasn't in a good mood when you rang.'

'No need to apologise, I shouldn't have contacted you. You were obviously still upset. Perfectly understandable.'

'Even so, you're the last person I want to upset.'

Things have been a bit awkward between us since the night when he asked me to stay overnight so his apology has made me feel that things might be getting back to normal between us.

'And I've had a rethink, I'd like to see my brother again.'

'Oh, I didn't expect that. What made you change your mind?'

'I spoke to Mum and she encouraged me to go for it.'

'Another surprise. The last time I spoke with her she was extremely cautious.'

'Yeah I know but she's also had a change of heart. She advised me to wear shoulder and shin pads and I think that in itself has encouraged us both.'

'That's weird because I was going to mention that to you the next time we talked. In fact I should've brought it up before meeting in the park. I'm sorry about that, it could've helped the situation.'

'No worries, that meeting was arranged quickly and I'm sure all your thoughts were totally focused on my hair. Now, the big question is where do we meet up this time?'

'How about a pub? Kieran likes beer and it generally makes him calmer.'

'Does it have to be a pub that doesn't serve food?'

'Not necessarily. If he has his dinner just before we go out then it's not so much of an issue, based on past experiences,' I reply.

'What about tomorrow at the pub I met Mum? The Victoria in Kings Cross.'

'Yep, no problem. Shall we say five? Whenever we go out he always wants to be back to StarLight by seven at the latest.'

'Well, judging from my last two outings with him that shouldn't be a problem but I'm hoping that tomorrow will be different. Don't you have to talk to him first?'

'Yes I do but hopefully he'll be OK. Can you do me a big favour and get him a couple of bars of Golden Crisp Irish chocolate? That's his favourite chocolate. The only place I know you can buy it is in an Irish shop called Crowley's on the high street in Kentish Town. I think it'll be a nice gesture, whether he appreciates it or not.'

'I'll go there now. Anything that'll help. By the way how did he get on at the charity shop today?'

'Not bad but he did tell a customer to piss off.'

'Well I'm glad it's just not me he slags off,' Ryan laughs, 'I'll see you tomorrow.'

'It's so good to hear that you're in a better mindset. Maybe sometime soon we can go out for a meal or a drink, without Kieran?' I ask.

'Nothing would please me more.'

I'm excited at the prospect of an social evening out with Ryan. I still haven't heard back from HR about the company policy on dating siblings of residents so I need to tread carefully.

As soon as I get off the phone with Ryan I head straight to Kieran's bedroom.

'Kieran, Ryan wants to have a drink with us tomorrow, would you like that?' I blurt out.

'Is he paying for my beers?' Kieran asks.

'Yes he will.'

'I want three beers.'

'OK that's no problem.' It's encouraging that he's talking about staying for three drinks.

I'm not going to discuss it any further. Three free beers seems to be a deal breaker.

I immediately text Ryan.

'Tomorrow's definitely on.'

'Third time lucky?' He replies.

'Yes, I think this time it will be.'

If this goes pear-shaped, I don't think there will be a fourth time.

CHAPTER THIRTY THREE: RYAN

I arrive at the pub half-an-hour early. After what happened the last time I'm not taking any chances.

I've nearly finished my pint when Kieran and Sienna arrive. Our first conversation is vital. It needs to get off on the right footing.

'Hello, Kieran. I've got a present for you,' I say to my brother as I hand him six Golden Crisp chocolate bars.

'Only six?' He says.

I'm tempted to laugh but I notice his serious expression so I refrain.

'I'll get you some more this week.'

'When exactly?' He replies.

'By Saturday and I'll bring them straight to you at StarLight.'

I expect another question but to my surprise he just nods.

'So what drink are you having?' I ask Kieran.

'What have they got?'

'The lagers are Fosters, Heineken and Peroni.'

'What else?'

'Guinness, Doom Bar, Ruddles, Smithwick's, Bulmers Cider…'

'Is that it?'

'Wine; red, white, Rose? The usual soft drinks – Coke, Lemonade?'

'What are you having?' Kieran asks me.

'Fosters.'

'Then I'll have half a pint of that Peroni lager. I like Italians even if they do sometimes piss me off when they get too excited, but they make lovely pizzas.'

'OK great. White wine?' I ask Sienna.

'Yes please.'

While I'm at the bar I reflect on the past couple of minutes. So far so good. OK, he did ask me to list every drink that this pub serves and worryingly I was able to successfully answer that without even looking at the bar taps but it's like walking a tightrope, so I decide to belatedly take Sienna's advice and resume the conversation on a safe topic – Bob Denny. I bring the drinks back to my brother and Sienna.

'I saw the video you did with Bob Denny. That was amazing,' I say to Kieran.

'Do you know his date of birth?'

'No, I don't.'

'So why are you so interested in him?' He asks.

'Because I know that you like him.'

'Kieran, just tell Ryan what happened at the gig?' Sienna gently intercepts.

'There's no point if he doesn't even know Bob's date of birth.'

'OK so instead why don't you tell your brother all about the wonderful work you did this morning?' Sienna suggests. I'm grateful that she hasn't pursued the Bob Denny conversation in case it agitates him further.

'I was told by the nice haircut lady that I'll have to deal with shitty underpants but instead I sorted out the DVDs so that was much better than I thought it was going to be.'

'That's good to hear,' I say.

'Do you still wear blue underpants?' He asks.

'I have many different coloured underpants and off the top of my head I think there's a couple of blue ones in there,' I reply, slightly embarrassed to be discussing my underpants inventory in front of Sienna.

'I have fifteen underpants, five blue, four black, two red, two grey and two white, but the blue ones weren't the ones that you left behind,' he informs me.

I'm tempted to carry on with the underpants conversation but how far can I go with that?

'Sienna told me you were fed up because I pinched and kicked you. Why was that?' Kieran asks me.

'Because it hurt me,' I could say an awful lot more but once again I hold back.

'You didn't mind it when you were sixteen and you're bigger and stronger now so what's the problem?'

'As you're also bigger and stronger it actually hurts more and although I'd prefer you didn't do it at all, if you feel you can't help yourself then there's nothing I can do about it.'

'Are you going to run away again for another fourteen years?'

'No, I'm not. I'm your brother and I'm going to try to make amends for my mistakes if you give me a chance.'

Kieran stands up, walks to the toilet and comes back with a handful of paper towels. He hands them to me and points to my upper right arm. Although he hasn't verbally informed me of his intentions I know exactly what's going to happen. I place the paper towels against my arm and straight away he gives me several hefty pinches there, again through gritted teeth. After he finishes he looks for a reaction and I remember Sienna telling me that when he used to do this to her in the early days of her involvement with him she over exaggerated her response which sometimes stopped him in his tracks. When I angrily shouted at him the last time he hit me it had no effect, but it's still worth a try.

'That fucking hurt,' I tell my brother as I'm holding my arm. He looks intently at me and then unbelievably gently strokes my arm. This action almost brings me to tears as it's the first sign of affection towards me since… well ever.

I glance at Sienna who smiles at me.

Kieran sips his beer without saying anything. I wasn't lying to him because it did hurt but as Mum told me yesterday the impact was less due to the combination of the shoulder pad and paper towels. It's manageable, which is a massive step forward. The fact that he went out of his way to get the paper towels speaks volumes.

'Kieran, what other celebrities do you like?' Sienna asks. I am grateful for her intervention as I'm too emotional to speak right now.

'I don't like famous people who are fat or have long hair, only ones that wear suits.'

'So do you have anyone in mind?' Sienna inquiries.

'Frank Sinatra. His voice is like eating a strawberry cheesecake and I never saw him wearing jeans or a t-shirt.'

'Wow, you're very young to know about Frank Sinatra,' she replies.

'Mum played his music all the time but his problem is that he's dead. He's the only dead singer that I like. But I didn't like his music when he got chunky.'

'Whenever I hear his music my mind goes back to when it was just me, you and Mum sitting in the living-room with one of Mum's many Sinatra records playing in the background. I didn't care for his music then but I do now. It's a happy memory,' I say to my brother, surprised by my sentimental admission and the fact that I do have a happy childhood memory.

Kieran stares at me but doesn't respond.

'What do you think of telephone directories?' Kieran asks me.

'To be honest I haven't really thought too much about them recently,' I reply.

'Because everyone now has a mobile phone they don't produce enough directories. I have all of the London British Telecom ones from 2004 to 2016. If I want the current ones I have to go online and order them. Those greedy bastards at British Telecom want bank notes for them now but I'm not going to do that. I don't like Yellow Pages because I'm not interested in contacting a plumber or hiring a car. I don't even drive so that's no use to me. I just like looking at where people live and what their phone numbers are. Sometimes I ring them up for a chat.'

'Are they people you know?'

'No, just random people.'

'And what do you talk about?'

'I always start off by asking who their favourite comedian is.'

'And what do they say?'

'Most of them just hang up but last week I got talking to an eighty-nine year old lady. She was telling all about that Hitler war. She didn't like him much because he bombed her local sweet shop. I told her it was probably a mistake.'

'And which comedian did she like?'

'Some bloke called Arthur Askey. I never heard of him so I hung up.'

'Do you like going to pubs?' I ask my brother.

'Only when there's no football match on the TV because it's too crowded and they're all very noisy which hurts my ears. I always tell them to shut up.'

'And how do they react to that?'

'Sometimes they tell me to fuck off so I tell those noisy shits to fuck off out of the pub.'

'Wow, that's confrontational.'

'Yes, it is and on a few occasions one or two of the guys have come to our table to confront him but when they notice his magical 'I have AUTISM' badge they apologise to him. This happened again last week and when the guy re-joined the football group he actually told them to keep the noise down,' Sienna tells me.

'Yeah, that was a shame cos I would've beaten the shit out of him,' Kieran adds.

Of that I have no doubt.

'I knew that there was no football on tonight so this was a safe bet,' Sienna says.

'Are you a football fan?' I ask Sienna.

'No, but I always check the fixture list before we go to the pub with Kieran. When he's really keen to go and there's a high profile match on we just have to face the consequences. It's hard to find a pub that he likes in this area that doesn't have Sky Sports.'

This night has been just perfect. I still can't get over Kieran handing me the paper towels and then stroking my arm afterwards. Such a simple gesture but it meant so much. Although he was irritated that I didn't know Bob Denny's date of birth, the conversation has been congenial. Perhaps I should take him for a beer every time we meet up?

'Do you want another beer?' I ask Kieran.

'What have they got?' He asks again.

Although it was only twenty minutes ago that I told him the complete list of beers I repeat them all to him again.

'OK, I'll have another Peroni,' he replies.

'I'll help you,' Sienna tells me as she follows me to the bar.

'What's changed?' I ask Sienna, as we're waiting for our drinks.

'Your guess is as good as mine but don't question it.'

'I'm not, it's just I haven't done anything different this time, well apart from the padding but that's invisible to him.'

'Maybe it took a couple of visits to get used to seeing you again? I've given him plenty of pep talks but as you know most of the time he just does his own thing. I was amazed when he gave you the paper towels. I didn't expect that. He's never done anything like that for me.'

'I feel privileged and, stroking my arm afterwards… I'm lost for words.'

'I know. I'd like to say we're turning the corner but without wishing to sound like the prophet of doom, it could all go pear-shaped at the drop of a hat,' she replies.

'Yeah, I mustn't get too carried away.'

We return to Kieran and I hand him his beer. He takes a couple of sips but then just stares in my direction. I've got to break the silence.

'Do you ever think about Dad?' I ask him and immediately regret saying it as this could easily set him off. Sienna told me several times to stick to safe topics and this certainly isn't safe.

'I sometimes dream about him. In my dreams Mum is telling us not to go near him as 'he'll eat the head off ya,' so I didn't talk much to him.'

I haven't heard that expression since I left home. Mum said it a lot, always in reference to my father but now it could easily apply to Kieran. Mum was born in Ireland but came over to England when she was sixteen years old. She was always coming up with these typically Irish sayings.

'Yeah, he was always so angry but you mustn't take it personally, he was like that to me and Mum too,' I tell my brother.

'Sienna told me that he isn't in a coffin yet so why doesn't he send me any presents?'

'I don't know. I haven't seen him since he left home,' I reply.

'Did he bugger off with a whore?'

'I don't think so.'

'I want to see him again,' Kieran says.

I look at Sienna who subtly shakes her head. I presume she's letting me know not to continue with this conversation so I take a sip of my beer and desperately try to think of something else to say.

'Who's your best friend at StarLight?' Is all I can come up with.

'Don't your ears work?' Kieran asks.

'What do you mean?'

'I want to see my dad. He owes me fifteen years of crisps as well as Christmas and birthday presents. I want you to contact him tomorrow,' he says.

I'm guessing from the tone in his voice that he means business and isn't going to be fobbed off.

'Does Mum know where he lives?' I ask Sienna.

'Yes, I think she does,' she replies.

Kieran is still looking intently at me.

'OK, I'll contact him tomorrow.'

'Fifteen years of crisps, I can't wait,' he says, smiling. That's actually the first time I've seen him smile since we've met up again.

Before coming here tonight I imagined many different scenarios on how the evening would pan out but not for one second did I think I would promise my brother that I'd contact our father again.

CHAPTER THIRTY FOUR: RYAN

'Why did you have to talk about your father? It was going so well,' Sienna asks me.

It's nine o'clock in the morning. I'm listening to her on my Bluetooth as I'm driving to a house just off the Holloway Road in North London to fix a boiler for an elderly couple. It's freezing and they have no heat so there's no way I can defer this job for another day, which I have been doing a lot of lately due to various commitments with Kieran. The older the customer the higher up on my priority list they become.

I hardly slept at all last night. The evening was an emotional rollercoaster. Kieran's attitude towards me seems to have changed. OK he did attack me but I have to accept that he's going to do this for an indefinite period. I now realise it's the price I have to pay if I'm to have a relationship with him. I am hoping that it will eventually peter out as it's mostly done with Sienna. Even after he dropped the bombshell about my father the rest of my time with him went relatively smoothly, even if some of the conversations were a little out there. He asked for my thoughts on my favourite pillow size and we also spent a long time discussing the different types of pens that are on the market. These are not exactly the most riveting conversations to most people but for Kieran to be talking to me in a calm manner was amazing. He told me that he preferred the *Friends* TV programme to fish and chips and then asked me which one I favoured. Although it was a slightly odd comparison I chose fish and chips. Kieran's favourite character in *Friends* is the apartment janitor – not the most obvious choice. He also informed me that he thought it was extremely silly of the cast to get their clothes wet in the opening fountain sequence. 'I'm sure that they all ended up with colds but they've only got themselves to blame,' he told me.

However once I asked him about our father he was extremely insistent that I contact him, so there's no way I can get out of it.

'So when are you going to ring your dad?' Sienna asks.

'I've got a boiler to fix right now but I'll do it after that. I'm so nervous. As you already know my so called father wants nothing to do with us so it's going to end up in disappointment, more for Kieran than myself. I have zero expectations but I'm worried that Kieran just won't understand. I'm furious with myself for bringing it up in the first place.'

'Have you spoken to your mum?'

'Yeah, as soon as I got home last night. She was really pleased when I told her how well the evening went with Kieran but not happy at all about the possibility of meeting good old George.'

'Was it a heated discussion?'

'No, but she was disappointed and couldn't see a way out of it. Even though it was me who asked about our arsehole father I didn't think for a second that it would lead to this.'

'I admit it took me by surprise as well.'

'I don't know how I'm even going to start off the conversation; 'Hi, Dad, remember me?''

'Can't you tell Kieran that you tried to contact him but the number Sally gave you was wrong?'

'No, Kieran told me when you went to the Ladies last night that if I don't get to speak to him then he will and I don't want that to happen.'

'Do you want me to talk to your father instead? It might be better coming from an outsider,' Sienna suggests.

'No thanks, it's something I need to do. I owe it to my brother. Sienna, I've got to go as I'm running late. I'll be in touch.'

'Good luck.'

I arrive at my destination a few minutes later and am greeted by a man who must be in his mid-eighties.

'Thanks so much for coming. Our normal plumber is inundated and won't be able to come until next week but we'll be dead by then if we don't get any heat,' he tells me with a kind smile.

'No worries, let's have a look at it.'

I enter the house and on my way to the boiler I'm greeted by his wife who is wearing a coat and a woolly hat. It doesn't take me long to realise that the reason the boiler isn't working is due to a frozen pipe. From past experience I know that it's a relatively easy fix and half-an-hour later the boiler is up and running.

'You're a miracle worker,' the man tells me. He's looking at me as if I've just told him he's won the lottery.

'How much do I owe you?' He asks.

'Nothing, just let your wife know that she can take her coat and hat off now.'

'Please let me pay you.'

'It's OK, I'm doing another job in this area so it's on my way. I'm glad to help.'

That was a lie. I don't normally waive my fee but one day I'll be old and be grateful if someone did me a kind turn. Maybe the Kieran experience has made me more compassionate?

They persuaded me to stay around for some tea and biscuits, that's something that rarely happens after finishing a job. They tell me their life history, how they met, why they couldn't have kids etc. He was a police officer but then told me that he was nervous about going out at night which I found very sad. However it was a lovely encounter and they were extremely grateful which made me feel better for doing a good deed.

The man's anxiety about leaving his house at night made me think about my father again. Does he feel the same? Has he now retired? Is he in good health? He must be in his sixties but he was a heavy smoker and liked a drink – did he continue with that lifestyle? Has age mellowed him or is he still the same selfish bastard that I once knew? There's so much I don't know about him.

I can't put off making that phone call any longer so I dial his house phone.

'Hello,' a female voice answers.

'Is George there?' I ask.

'Who's calling?'

'Ryan, his son. There's no emergency, no-one has died, I just want to speak to him.'

'Hold on,' I can faintly hear a conversation, probably from another room. A couple of minutes later she returns.

'Can he ring you back? He's just finishing his lunch and then has to take his medicine.'

'So his lunch is more important than speaking to his son? A son that he hasn't bothered to contact for over fifteen years.'

She doesn't respond.

'I'll ring you every hour until he comes to the phone and if that doesn't work I'll visit him myself.'

'Just hold on,' she wearily tells me again.

I nervously wait a few more minutes.

'There's no need to be so rude to my wife. She said I'd ring you back, didn't she?'

'And there I was thinking that this was going to be an emotional reunion.'

'OK, let's start again, shall we? Why are you ringing me? Is Sally OK?' He asks.

'She's fine, not that you give a shit. Do you ever reflect on how you were so fucking cruel to her?'

'Yes I do.'

'Don't lie to me. If you were so remorseful why didn't you ever apologise to her?'

He doesn't answer.

'Your silence says it all but I want to keep this conversation as brief as possible. My brother, Kieran, remember him? Anyway he wants to see you because he needs all the backdated Christmas and birthday presents for the last fifteen years. You know the ones you never bothered sending to your autistic son. So if you can send me cheque for say one thousand pounds or a bank transfer for that amount you won't hear from us again. Deal? I know you're not interested in seeing him so I'll make up some excuse to get you off the hook.'

Again he doesn't respond.

'I've done the maths, that's about thirty-five pounds for each present, don't you think Kieran deserves that? But what both of your sons didn't deserve was a father who didn't care one fuck about his parental responsibilities. You were a fucking useless father and don't get me started about the way you treated Mum. You were not only unfaithful to her throughout your so called marriage but unbelievably you flaunted your sordid affairs in front of her. You are one evil bastard. So what have you got to say about that?'

'It's something I've regretted.'

'Oh fuck off. Don't pay me lip service. Anyway how are you going to pay, cheque or bank transfer?'

'Neither, I'll give you cash.'

'What do you mean?'

'Come down here on Saturday with Kieran and Sally and I'll pay you.'

'Oh I get it, you've moved house and you're going to lead us on a wild goose chase as some sort of sick joke. That'll appeal to your warped sense of humour.'

'Helen, can you tell Ryan where we live please?' George asks his wife.

'We've lived at the same address for the last fifteen years, twenty-five Colmer Road, Boscombe, Bournemouth, I'll give you directions if you like,' Helen tells me.

'OK, what time do you want us to come?' I ask, still wary that he's stringing me along.

'Whatever time's good for you, just let me know,' my father replies.

'OK, please don't play any tricks because Kieran will go berserk if you do. I'm just warning you if he gets angry he may well lash out and despite the fact that you're a nasty piece of work I don't want him to hurt you.'

'There's no tricks. There's a lot I need to get off my chest.'

'You and me both. Oh and by the way he's expecting a box or two of crisps as well; OK?'

'See you on Saturday,' he replies before hanging up.

From my car viewpoint I look out at a crowded North London High Street. Most of the shoppers are dressed in thick coats and scarfs and seem in a hurry to reach their destination to get out of the cold but all I'm thinking about is the conversation I've just had with my father. It was bizarre and not what I expected. Even when I let rip several times about how he neglected his family in such a brutal manner he didn't try to defend himself, in fact he even told me that he regretted his actions. However when I pressed him on why he never expressed his guilt to my mother he didn't answer so I have my doubts on whether he's telling me the truth. I was expecting a confrontational discussion but that never happened and I'm amazed that he not only agreed to pay Kieran one thousand pounds he actually invited us all over to his house to collect the payment. I have no idea how Mum is going to react to all of this but I'm pretty sure she has no burning desire to see him again.

Despite the bewildering conversation I was pleased that I told him some home truths; they were long overdue.

I ring my mother.

'I've been waiting to hear from you, how did it go?' She asks before I have a chance to speak.

'Just before I rang him I thought of an arbitrary monetary value that he owed Kieran for all the lost presents and just came up with a thousand pounds. Thinking that he would just tell me to piss off I had psyched myself for the inevitable confrontation but he agreed to pay without protest. However, what really threw me was when he asked us all to come down on Saturday and he'll hand over the cash then.'

'I don't believe it, do you trust him?'

'Normally I would say definitely not but he seemed different...calmer but I'm still confused. That invitation includes you.'

'Really? I'm not going and I'm not sure I want Kieran there either.'

'He has to be. If nothing else it'll give him closure with his father, whatever the outcome.'

'What else did he say?'

'Not a lot. Helen answered the phone and went away to get him but she came back saying he'd ring me later as he was finishing off his lunch and then taking his medicine, which I found very strange. I'm trying to understand his thought process; his son suddenly contacts him again after fifteen years you'd think something was up, wouldn't you? Instead he was irritated because I was abrupt with Helen, but that was because I thought he was fobbing me off.'

'Do you still think that?' She asks.

'I don't know. It was the weirdest conversation that I've ever had with him and that's saying something.'

'This is all moving so fast, I'm a nervous wreck,' my mother tells me.

'Please don't be. We're together again and I had a nice evening with Kieran so there's some positives. Even if it doesn't work out with that bastard I'll soften the blow and pay Kieran the thousand pounds myself. I'm hoping he'll be happy with that.'

'There's no need...'

'Yes there is, it's the least I can do for him.'

'But of course there's more at stake than just the monetary value. How will it affect Kieran if it goes pear-shaped?' My mother asks.

'We have no choice now, it's a risk we have to take.'

After speaking to Mum I contact Sienna and re-iterate my father's conversation to her. She's also concerned about the impact on Kieran but overall she thought that it was a positive move that he actually agreed to meet us. She's definitely a glass half-full person.

Just as the conversation is petering out she asks me around for dinner tomorrow night at her flat, which was yet another unexpected twist and I accepted of course.

After spending the rest of the day fixing boilers, more frozen pipes and a waterlogged bathroom I'm pleased to be back in my flat with a chilled glass of white wine listening to Ray Davies who is letting me know about a chap who appears to be a dedicated follower of fashion.

What an unbelievable day. To be invited around to Sienna's was a lovely surprise. I have made the first move in all of my previous female relationships but not so far with Sienna. Just as I think we're developing more than just a professional relationship she keeps her distance so I don't know if it will ever progress any further than it is right now. Being Kieran's carer does complicate things. How would he react if we started dating? Yet another risk but I'm getting way ahead of myself here. I enjoy her company immensely and I admire her so much for not only the care and devotion that she has shown to my brother, despite the most difficult of circumstances, but also the fact that against all odds she has reunited me with my mother and brother. Whatever happens from here on in I'll be forever grateful to her for doing that.

But then my thoughts turn to my father. In three days' time I will see him again for the first time in fifteen years. There's so much I want to tell him, all of which he won't want to hear but I will have to pick my moments very carefully as I'll have Kieran with me.

I never thought I'd ever see my father again. I had no desire to and although I'm nervous, I'm glad I've got this opportunity because the likelihood is I'll never see him again after Saturday.

CHAPTER THIRTY FIVE:
SIENNA

'Fifteen years of crisps, I can't wait,' Kieran tells me, 'but I wonder how the 2008 crisps will taste now.'

'Kieran, you can't buy 2008 crisps now but your father might give some money and you can buy some crisps with that,' I reply, just in case my father thought I was joking about replenishing the crisps.

'He usually got me two packets of crisps a week so that's one hundred and four crisps packets he owes me for 2008, one hundred and four crisps packets for 2009, one hundred ...'

'OK, Kieran, I get what you're saying but that'll be over a thousand crisps packets, there's no way you can eat that amount.'

'Although he left on the sixth of November 2008 I'm counting that as a full year because I stayed up all night waiting for him while he disappeared with his whore so that makes the total one thousand, five hundred and sixty packets of crisps that he owes me. I'm also counting this year as a full year.'

'When you meet your father you can discuss that with him,' I inform Kieran. I'm washing my hands over the substantial crisps debt.

'How do you feel about seeing your father again?' I ask, keen to change the subject.

'I want to know if he still wears white t-shirts and whether he's got any hair left. Anyway will he know who I am?'

'Of course he will, don't worry about that.'

'What's the name of that tart that he's with now?'

'She's not a tart, and her name is Helen.'

I'm assuming she's not a tart.

'Can I spit at her?'

'No you can't.'

'But I spit at Mum.'

'And that's wrong. I've told you that so many times.'

'It makes me feel better.'

'But it's still wrong.'

This comes back to the repetitive OCD behaviour that some autistic people have to do in order to cope with a stressful and bewildering world that they live in.

As Kieran is so unpredictable I have no idea how Saturday will pan out. Will he be the tense and aggressive Kieran that I saw on his first two encounters with Ryan or slightly more subdued as he was at the last meeting?

I wonder why his father readily agreed to meet up. Ryan mentioned that his father was regretful over his past mistakes but wasn't convinced he was telling the truth. If Kieran gets his thousand pounds he'll be delighted but I do worry about the long term implications of this meeting. However Kieran has suddenly got the bit between his teeth about seeing his father so the Saturday get together is inevitable.

Although Ryan, Sally and myself all have concerns, Kieran is just focused on his one thousand, five hundred and fifty-six packets of crisps and whether Helen is a prostitute. It should be an interesting family reunion.

I'm not sure why Kieran keeps questioning Helen's occupation. Maybe he does remember arguments between his parents about his father's infidelities.

From what Ryan has told me it sounds like Sally won't be there, which is perfectly understandable as it could turn into a volatile gathering but I also wonder if it might give her some resolution on her turbulent marriage.

It's all a minefield.

'How would you like to spend tomorrow evening with Ryan? Just you and him,' I ask Kieran.

He looks at me but doesn't respond.

'I'll drop you off and pick you up but it'll be nice if you could spend some time alone with your brother. You can go wherever you want and Ryan will pay for everything.' I'm hoping that the monetary incentive will swing it in my favour.

'But it's the StarLight disco night tomorrow and I don't know if he likes music.'

'He does.'

'What music does he listen to?'

'He saw Elton John in concert a couple of months ago.'

'Every time I see photos of that man he's wearing a different pair of spectacles and they're always in different colours. Does he keep losing them? I bet he's not happy about wasting his petrol allowance driving to *Specsavers* to get a new pair every time he mislays them? He's very careless. I wonder if he ever forgets to bring his piano to his concerts. No I don't like forgetful musicians.'

I won't bother with a counter argument.

'Ryan likes the Beatles, what do you think of their music?'

'Two of them are dead so why do I keep hearing their songs all the fucking time on the radio?'

'Their music will last forever,' I tell Kieran.

'No their music should've only been played when all four of them were alive.'

I'm impressed that he knows that there were four Beatles. Let's hope that the music tomorrow night doesn't include any dead or careless musicians.

'So are you OK to spend tomorrow evening with Ryan?'

'Yeah, but I'm going to leave my money in my bedroom, he can get the notes out of his wallet for my beers.'

I completely forgot about the StarLight disco. I'm just so wrapped up with everything that's been happening in Kieran's family. There are a number of StarLight residential care homes and every three months or so a disco is held for the residents from all the houses and their families. I really enjoy these evenings as it's just so heart-warming and humbling to witness these special needs adults enjoying a normal social activity.

I think it'll also be good for Ryan to witness how the other residents interact with each other as well as their own families. Of course Ryan doesn't know anything about this yet but I doubt he'll refuse after Kieran agreed to having his brother accompany him for the evening. If Ryan has anything planned I'm sure he'll cancel it.

'I was pleased that you got on better with your brother the other day. How did you feel after seeing him?' I ask.

'My mind felt nice after those beers.'

'It was good of you to give him the paper towels to cover his arm. Why did you do that?'

'The beers told my brain not to bruise his arm too much.'

I nod. Does that mean that every Ryan/Kieran get together has to involve alcohol?

'Can we go on the Piccadilly tube line today?' Kieran asks.

'OK, where is it you want to go?' I reply.

'I want to stay on the Piccadilly line as the tube calms me but I don't want to go into a carriage with thousands of people because they always look pissed off. If they're so fed up why don't they do something else like swimming or horse riding? I just like the colour of the Piccadilly line.'

'Do you mean the blue colour on the tube map?'

'Yeah, what else did you think I was talking about? I can tell you're really confused. Do you need me to explain how the colour system works on the underground map?' He replies, a little irritated.

'That's OK, give me a few minutes and we'll get going. I just want to check my emails.'

'Oh forget it, my momentum has been lost now,' Kieran replies.

'I can look at my emails later.'

'Nah, I've lost interest. There's no point going on the underground if you don't understand how it all works. It'll be a waste of time.'

Kieran's mood can change dramatically over something quite insignificant. Well insignificant to me but obviously not for him. I do understand that the colour of the Piccadilly tube line is blue but when I asked for clarification on what he was trying to convey he got annoyed. Sometimes I pursue a conversation like this to try and clear up a misunderstanding but he's edgy, so on this occasion I leave him be.

'Seeing as you're clueless about the London Underground set up, can we go Kings Cross railway station instead?' Kieran asks.

'What town do you want to travel to?'

'I'm not interested in going anywhere.'

'So you just want to go the station?'

'Yeah, I love the sweet shop Dunny's on the station concourse. The cans of coke are the coldest I've ever had. I want to buy four cans. I'll have to put them in a bag because my hands don't like holding anything that's chilly but my mouth just loves icy drinks.'

'Are you sure you don't want to get on a train?'

'Nah, Tuesdays are not good days for train journeys.'

I don't question Kieran's unexplained thoughts on Tuesday train journeys. To avoid escalating his impatience even further we leave StarLight within a few minutes and make our way to Kings Cross station.

Trains are an obsession with a lot of autistic children and adults. A lot of this stems from their seemingly endless fixation with Thomas The Tank Engine. A couple of years ago I went on holiday to Boston with my then boyfriend, Philip. During our stay I visited one of the most renowned autistic schools in the world, the Higashi School. Under normal circumstances, if I required a tour of the school I would have to book it well in advance but after speaking to the Higashi school on the phone the day after we arrived in Boston a very helpful lady told me to come straight down. Philip didn't go. Such was his interest in my career he decided to play eighteen holes of golf on his own. I was overwhelmed by the way the courses were tailored meticulously to the understanding level of the autistic pupil and the facilities were also extremely impressive. The dedication of the staff there was heartwarming and overall it ticked all the boxes.I could see how Kieran, Jamie, Billy and Nicky would thrive in that environment but I was a little shocked at the price of the schooling. At the time of my visit the tuition was $32,000 and the boarding was $90,000. Geraldine was the lady who kindly showed me around and she told me that a number of the British families were constantly fund raising throughout the year to afford these school fees and some had even sold their houses. All quite humbling.

I asked Geraldine if the American children and adults were also obsessed with Thomas and she told me that it was the top fictional character they identified with. I know that Jamie and Billy play their Thomas DVDs every day but Kieran doesn't possess any and is not really into trains as much as his fellow residents. Jamie and Billy regularly inform me that London Underground trains are not 'proper trains.'

Despite his reluctance to handle cold items, Kieran spends ages feeling several cans of coke at Dunny's before deciding on the chosen four. He then puts his gloves back on before putting them on the counter.

'Why aren't you wearing gloves?' He asks the cashier.

'It's cold but I'm working indoors.'

'I'm amazed that you grabbed those cans and didn't flinch.'

'It's my job.'

'You're a brave man. How the hell do you get those cans so goddamn cold?'

'I dunno.'

'You must know.'

'Probably something to do with the temperature setting on the fridge,' the cashier replies.

'You're just guessing now, aren't you?' Kieran asks.

'OK, Kieran, just pay the man and we'll get going,' I interrupt.

'You don't really know what you're doing, admit it,' Kieran continues.

'Actually I do. I've been in this job seven years so I think I've got the hang of it by now.'

'Do they pay you?'

'Of course they do,' he replies with a sigh.

'In bank notes or biscuits?'

'Kieran is autistic,' I explain and should have mentioned it five minutes ago.

The cashier smiles at us.

'Why the fuck are you selling cigarettes? Don't you know they kill people?' Kieran shouts after glimpsing a cigarette packet that was visible in the cupboard behind the cashier.

'They're just part of our stock.'

'Walt Disney died from smoking too much and I loved *Bambi*. You didn't sell him any cigarettes, did you?'

I hand the cashier a fiver (Kieran didn't seem in too much of a hurry to put his hand in his pocket) and we exit the store before the cashier has a chance to let Kieran know that he wasn't in any way responsible for Walt Disney's death.

Just another surreal conversation with a bewildered member of the public.

Kieran is calmer throughout the rest of the day and it seemed to coincide with purchasing his cans of coke. So every time he's stressed out, does that mean I'll have to take him to Dunny's? I'm not sure that cashier will be best pleased to see us again.

I keep checking my emails to see if HR have responded to my inquiry about dating Ryan (although I didn't specifically mention his name), but so far there's been no answer. I did have a brief chat with our StarLight manager, Debbie, and she thought that it shouldn't be an issue and that she didn't have a problem with it but I still have to wait for the official response. As I'm seeing Ryan tonight it would've been nice to have it resolved, not that I'm planning a night of wild, no-holds-barred sex, but you never know.

I'm preparing Ryan's favourite meal – a traditional roast. I feel nervous about inviting him to my flat as it somehow feels like the relationship has gone onto another level, when in reality it hasn't.

Just as I'm taking the bottle of wine out of the fridge, Ryan arrives. He's clearly made an effort – wearing trendy, tight jeans with a navy blue shirt. I still can't get used to his short, dyed hair. I prefer it longer and I'm sure he does too but needs must.

I pour us both a glass of wine and we sit down for our meal.

'It looks delicious, thanks so much for inviting me,' he says.

'As I've been around yours so many times it's only fair I return the compliment.'

'How was Kieran today? Did he mention me at all?'

'He's been OK. We went to Kings Cross station just to visit a sweet shop and he more or less accused the cashier of causing Walt Disney's death by serving him cigarettes.'

'I'm not sure I follow…'

'Don't worry about it, all in a day's work. But your name did crop up in conversation as I'm planning a social event for you tomorrow.'

'OK, where are we going?'

'Not us, just you and Kieran. Are you a good dancer?'

'Absolute shit, why?'

'You're going to the StarLight disco tomorrow night with your brother. Just you and him and of course all the residents from the other houses. I'm afraid you can't get out of it as I've already told Kieran.'

'And he was OK with it?'

'Yes, as long as you get him his beers.'

'Why don't you come along as well?' Ryan asks.

'You need an evening alone with your brother. Admittedly you'll probably be accompanied by Abba.'

'Won't the music defeat the whole objective of this?'

'What do you mean?'

'It might be difficult holding a conversation.'

'You're not going to a Metallica gig, it'll be a welcome distraction for him. He's usually in a good mood at these discos, he likes music. Anyway it'll give you an opportunity to see him interacting with his peers. But if it all gets too much for either of you just ring me and I'll make my way there.'

'Does he have a girlfriend?'

'No and as far as I can tell he never has. He shows no interest. I suppose you could say he's asexual.'

'I feel ashamed even asking you that question at this late stage.'

'No, I should've mentioned it myself. I'm pretty sure all the other residents are too.'

'Because of their special needs it must be difficult to maintain a girlfriend/boyfriend type relationship,' Ryan says.

'I always find it amusing when a middle-aged person refers to their partner as boyfriend or girlfriend. Yes, of course these relationships exist in the autistic world but personally I haven't seen it. It's even rarer for an autistic person to be with someone that's considered normal.'

'That's a shame. They need companionship more than most.'

'Getting back to the disco, what are your thoughts about going?' I ask.

'I'm nervous. You're my security blanket. You always know the right thing to say and do but I need to stand up for myself and not rely on you all the time. I feel slightly reassured after the last meeting but that could be a false dawn.'

'There's only one way to find out.'

'Talking about relationships, have you heard anything from Philip since you split?'

'No, but I didn't expect to.'

'Has that put you off dating?'

'Why, are you offering?' I ask without hesitation. I wish I hadn't drank that second glass of wine too quickly.

There's an awkward silence.

'I didn't mean…' I stutter.

'No, it's OK, I'd love to take you out for a date, a meal, call it what you like. Actually you do owe me a day out in Brighton or have you conveniently forgotten about that?'

'How could I? You remind me practically every time we meet up. But yes we have to fix a date. How about next Saturday? I believe you've got something on this Saturday.'

'Don't remind me. I'm shitting myself thinking about the next forty-eight hours. When we were growing up we never went out as a family. I'm assuming that was because money was tight, so spending any social time alone with Kieran is really a first for me. I just hope he doesn't want me to dance because I dance like David Brent in that *Office* episode; not a pretty sight, especially after a couple of drinks. And of course meeting my father after fifteen years, I just can't get my head around that.'

'Ryan, can I be totally honest with you?'

'Go ahead.'

'I would love to go out with you and I truly mean that. You've been through so much in your life but you still had the courage, after some persuasion, to see Kieran and Sally again even though it was a massive risk. Sally and I have talked a lot about Kieran regressing to his old behaviours but if those reunions went pear-shaped it would've had a damaging effect on you as well. I underestimated that. What I'm trying to say is that I think you're amazing and would love to get to know you better but here's the kicker, I'm not sure if it's against the company rules to date a resident's sibling. I've inquired about it with HR but they haven't come back yet. They don't rush for anyone.'

'You actually contacted HR about dating me?' He asks.

'Yes I did,' I reply.

'I'm surprised. I knew we got on well but I didn't think you were interested in taking it further.'

'I think you've just heard that I am.'

He leans forward to kiss me but I hold him off.

'I'm sorry, Ryan, I don't want to start something that I might have to stop. We both could get hurt.'

'I get what you're saying but who will know if we start going out with each other? We can be discreet,' Ryan replies.

'I know that we can probably get away with it, for a period of time anyway, but I don't want to take that risk. My job is everything to me.'

'This is 2023, surely the rules can't be that draconian?'

'I hope not but until I get the official word...'

'OK, let's wait but I just want to say that I've never felt this way about anyone before and I'm not spinning you a line, it's the truth. You're just wonderful and that Philip character must be an absolute dickhead for letting you go but I'm glad he did. Please ring me the moment you hear from HR.'

'You look disappointed and I am too, it's very frustrating but I'm quietly confident that it'll all work out and of course I'll let you know as soon as I know myself.'

Another uncomfortable silence.

'I really didn't expect this evening to unfold like this,' I tell Ryan.

CHAPTER THIRTY SIX: RYAN

I'm on my way to the StarLight disco.

I've been feeling anxious throughout the day. I can't stop thinking about my evening with Sienna. I was surprised and delighted when she revealed that she would like to go out with me but that joyful moment soon evaporated when she told me that she'd have to get the all clear from work. Logically I would hope that in this day and age it shouldn't be an issue but who knows? She made it quite clear that her job is more important than developing our relationship, although that's disappointing to hear I do understand where she's coming from. If our relationship never advances to the next level it will so difficult seeing her whenever I pick up Kieran at StarLight, that's assuming that my relationship with Kieran continues to evolve.

The thought that my involvement with Sienna will just be at a professional level makes me very sad.

Another cause of anxiety is the prospect of spending an evening with Kieran without Sienna's support.

I arrive at the hall on time but it's already very crowded. Obviously punctuality is very important in the autistic word as I found out to my cost. Most of the revellers are dancing to the song *Agadoo*. It's obviously a crowd favourite, personally I think it's an absolutely shit song but I'm clearly in the minority. I notice Kieran sitting at a table that is furthest away from the dance floor. There are three other guys with him but nobody is talking. Oh well in for a penny...

'How are you, Kieran? Are you enjoying the music?'

'Not yet.'

'What's the name of the group that sings this one?' I ask.

'They call themselves Black Lace and I haven't found out why. I google every song that comes on and the Wikipedia info will decide whether or not I enjoy the song.'

'So what's your verdict on this one?'

'There's a bloke who used to play for Black Lace called Alan Barton but he died in 1995 so I'll have nothing to do with them. Dead singers are wasting my time, apart from Frank Sinatra.'

A couple of days ago Kieran recalled a childhood memory of Mum playing Sinatra's records. This happens to all of us but I'm happy that Kieran has the same capacity to fondly remember that moment in the past.

'Have you danced yet?' I ask Kieran.

'Until those dancers up there stop frolicking all over the place I'm going nowhere near them.'

I'm relieved to hear that. The pressure to dance is off, for the time being.

'What's everyone drinking? This Ryan bloke is buying the drinks all night,' Kieran proclaims.

I'm not sure I agreed to that but it's a small price to pay for keeping the peace. I take the order of one lager, two cokes and a small glass of water without ice, lemon or lime. Killian is the only one drinking alcohol which I assume means that either the others just don't drink alcohol or they're on medication. Killian hasn't taken Ritalin since he was sixteen.

'My name's Jamie. I was born on the fifth of April 1996. That was a Friday. I thought I'd tell you that before you ask me. I love Michael McIntyre, especially when he wears suits but I can't ride a bicycle. Can you?' Jamie informs me as I arrive back with a tray of drinks. Nobody offered to give me a hand but judging from Kieran's self-centred nature this doesn't come as a surprise. Their needs are paramount, everyone else can take a run and jump.

'I can but I haven't for quite a while.'

'Can you teach me?'

'If you want me to then yes I will.'

'When?'

'I'll speak to Sienna about that.'

'Are you the bloke that Kieran beat the shit out of?' Jamie asks.

'My name's Ryan, I'm Kieran's brother. Yes we did have a slight disagreement but we're the best of friends now, aren't we, Kieran?'

Kieran stands up and gives me a couple of hefty pinches on my neck which hurt.

'What did you do that for?' I angrily ask my brother.

'I like the neck skin, it's tender,' he replies.

'If you have to pinch me can you do it on my arms or legs please?'

'But there are so many other parts of the body that my pinching fingers haven't explored yet.'

Does this mean I have to wear a neck brace now, in addition to shin and shoulder pads, dyed hair and no hair?

Kieran continues to read all about Black Lace, seemingly not bothered about the pain he just inflicted, almost as if it's a daily ritual for him, which I suppose it is. I'm disappointed but I've got to deal with it, both physically and mentally.

'My name's Billy and I'm five feet and nine inches.'

'Hello, Billy, how are you?'

'What do you mean?'

'How are you feeling today?' I ask.

'6.25 out of ten.'

'That's sort of good, isn't it?'

'It was higher. Before you arrived it was eight.'

'Do I make you feel anxious?'

'Yes. You don't have the autistic bug that we've all got,' Billy says as he points at his table companions.

Kieran has never mentioned to me that he is autistic but Billy's admission makes me wonder if he also aware of his own special needs.

'Just because I'm not autistic doesn't mean you should feel worried. Is there anything I can do to make you feel better?'

'Yeah, go home,' Billy calmly tells me.

'He can't go home as he has all the cash for the drinks,' Kieran chips in.

'Oh, OK then, but I'm nervous around normal people,' Billy replies.

'How did you know that I'm not autistic?' I ask Billy.

'Because you bought everyone a drink.'

'You can buy the next drinks if it makes you feel better.'

'Piss off, I'm not wasting my money on you.'

I know that Kieran is tight with his money and it seems that Billy is too but I don't remember reading anything about it being an autistic trait. I think it's a Kieran and Billy trait.

'And what's your name?' I ask the other guy sitting next to Kieran.

He stares at me but doesn't say anything.

'Are you enjoying the music?' I ask him, undeterred.

He grits his teeth and hits his forehead forcibly with his fist. I'm guessing that he's non-verbal. As I don't want to upset him further I don't pursue the conversation.

'I can see a lot of families here, so where are yours?' I ask both Jamie and Billy.

'We don't know our families anymore. I haven't see my parents or my brother since 2006 and Billy hasn't seen his family since 2008. They know where I live because I get a Christmas card from my mother but nobody visits us,' Jamie tells me.

I could cry at the thought of these guys not seeing their families but then again who am I to criticise anyone?

They really are alone in this world.

My urge is to give them both a hug but I know that physical contact is another cause of anxiety in the autistic world, so I refrain.

As I've chatted more to Jamie and Billy it's time to engage with my brother but as Abba's *Dancing Queen* is now playing it's Kieran who speaks first.

'At last, a group where everyone's alive,' he proclaims.

'Are you looking forward to the trip to Bournemouth?' I ask, deliberating leaving out the person we're going to visit there.

'It's eighty-seven miles from StarLight to Bournemouth and it's going to take two hours and thirty-two minutes but that's only if you drive properly. Have you passed your driving test?' He asks.

'Yes, I have.'

'What date was that?'

'I can't remember the exact date but it was in August 2015. I'll show you my full driving licence tomorrow,' I say, anticipating his next question.

'If there's no police cars around making a racket with their sirens and flashing their silly lights can we just go through the red traffic lights? We'll get to Bournemouth quicker and the other cars won't mind.'

'I'm afraid I always have to stop when the lights are red, that's the law.'

'I'm sure if we explain the crisps situation to the police they'll be OK about it,' he says.

'No, only members of the Royal family, the Pope, the American President, the Prime Minister, Heads of State and the like have that permission.'

'Can't you apply for one of those jobs?'

'It's not as simple as that,' I reply.

'Yes it is but I can see that you're obsessed with stopping at the lights so I'll just have to wait longer for my crisps.'

'Are you enjoying yourself?' I ask in an attempt to divert him away from the traffic lights discussion.

'I've been here fifty-eight minutes. I felt a bit depressed listening to the shit music for the first twenty-one minutes but after I started drinking that second beer my brain felt better and now Abba's music is on my brain's mood is improving even more.'

I was afraid that he might say that my arrival put him is a bad frame of mind so I'm relieved at his response.

'How do you feel about me seeing you again after all these years?' I ask, upping the ante.

'You arrived on time today and I can see your ears now so that makes me calmer.'

For the next few minutes I don't attempt at keeping the conversation flowing as I'm overcome with emotion. I realise that if somebody had genuinely complimented the visibility of my ears I would have thought they were off their trolley but right now it's the best compliment I could receive. We've come a long way since that first encounter at the restaurant when he was so aggressive. I'm getting used to some of his autistic ways but I know that I have to tread very carefully in everything I say to him and I don't think that's ever going to change.

'I also like that your wallet is full of bank notes,' he adds.

I'm not trying to buy his affections but I owe him a lot and not only in monetary terms.

Shortly afterwards a woman approaches our table.

'And how are we all doing?' She asks.

'That DJ is crap. He's talks too much and smiles all the time. I think he's a bit mad,' Kieran says.

'Being upbeat is his job if you pardon the pun,' she replies.

Kieran looks confused but then as the crap DJ plays a Steps record he immediately accesses Wikipedia. Given his obsession with dead people I'm expecting him to like Steps as I think they're all alive.

'My name's Debbie, I'm the manager of StarLight and you must be Ryan.'

'Yes, that's right,' I reply, standing up to shake her hand.

'It looks like you're a temporary staff member tonight,' she says as she looks at the table occupants.

'I'm only too pleased to help out,' I reply

'Sienna speaks very highly of you so I was reassured that they were in good hands but if you have any issues there's plenty of staff around to help. I'm so pleased that you're reunited with Kieran; he needs you,' she tells me.

'I'm ashamed that I've left it this long to get in contact with him. As you probably already know this has all been instigated by Sienna; she's been incredible.'

'Yes, she's done a sterling job.'

'Speaking of Sienna, I'm not sure how much detail she's told you but we both want our relationship to be more than just a professional one, however she's extremely reluctant to take it further in case it goes against company rules. What are your thoughts on that?' I ask.

'The last time I spoke to her she still hadn't heard back from HR, is that still the case?'

'Yes.'

'I must admit I haven't come across this situation before. If it was up to me it wouldn't be an issue but that decision is out of my hands. Without wishing to be the prophet of doom I think she would've heard from HR by now if it wasn't a problem but don't take that as gospel.'

That wasn't the response that I was hoping for.

CHAPTER THIRTY SEVEN: RYAN

It's half past five in the morning and I'm wide awake. I've only had a couple of hours sleep as I've got a lot on my mind. The prospect of seeing my father again is something I'm not looking forward to. If Kieran hadn't instigated this there is no way I'd be contacting my father. I only associate him with my traumatic childhood. I think for some strange reason he has resented me; he certainly took no interest in me. At least he gave Kieran the odd packet of crisps, I got nothing from him. I'm certain that Mum chose my birthday and Christmas presents, he didn't have a clue what presents I wanted. But I'm going through this painful process to please my brother but will he be happy seeing his father again? The money will help, that's if my father is true to his word which I have my doubts, but what will the long term impact of this visit have on Kieran? Only time will tell.

I am, however, determined to offload all my grievances on him. I actually wrote them all down the other day as I don't want to leave anything out. I'm not afraid of him anymore. He's an older man now, therefore not so intimidating. For the first time I hope to have the upper hand in our fractured relationship.

But it's not just the prospect of meeting my father that caused my lack of sleep. Throughout the night I reflected on the conversation I had with Debbie when she expressed her doubts on whether HR will give the go ahead to further pursue my relationship with Sienna. When Sienna first mentioned this last week I was disappointed but believed that this type of draconian rule did not exist in 2023, but now I'm having doubts. There's no way I'd ever ask Sienna to change jobs, I envy her passion for her work. I wish I felt the same way about my job but for me it's just a way of paying the bills. Waiting to find out the outcome is doing my head in.

However on a more positive note my evening with Kieran was a success. It didn't start well after his attack on my neck which I found scary and invasive and if that continues I will definitely need to wear protection. Would it be just easier to get dressed as a mummy every time I see him? However the rest of the evening went as well as I could have expected. He relaxed more and began to enjoy some of the music although he kept me updated on why he didn't like some of the tunes; the usual statement on dead musicians, vocals too loud (he hates Noddy Holder), long hair, silly clothes, too many musicians in the band, too smiley, too happy, the length of the song ('if it goes past three minutes and twenty seconds I get bored' – that does rule out a lot of songs), ginger hair (sorry, Ed), etc but the conversations were not confrontational. It felt good to effectively be in charge of a group of autistic adults. It gave me confidence and once again I've got Sienna to thank for her foresight. She hasn't put a foot wrong throughout all of this process. At various times I just couldn't see a positive outcome but she kept persevering, finding different ways to approach whatever scenario occurred. I owe her everything.

My thoughts are interrupted by the ringing tone on my mobile. Although it's not unusual to be called at this hour due to some emergency work issue I'm startled to see it's my mother whose calling.

'Is everything OK?' I ask her.

'Yes it is. I'm sorry to disturb you so early but I've just got on a train and wondered if you could pick me up at Kings Cross at around eight-thirty?'

'Of course. Are you going to Bournemouth with us?'

'Yes I am. For the past few days I've hardly slept, not knowing what to do for the best but yesterday I finally decided I need to be there to support my sons but also to let that piece of shit know some unpleasant truths that I've kept inside of me for way too long. I need closure.'

'I'm delighted that you're coming, I think you've made the right decision,' I tell her.

'Will Sienna be with us?'

'Yes she will. She didn't want to initially, she thought it was a personal family situation but I managed to persuade her. She may well be a calming influence should the conversations get too heated.'

'Absolutely. What time is he expecting us?'

'Between twelve and one. I texted him last night but he didn't reply.'

'Good, the sooner we get there the better. My train back is at eight.'

'Wow, that's a busy day for you. You can stay at mine if you want.'

'Thanks for the offer, Ryan, but no. I need to get back to Robert. He was desperate to come with me but I didn't want to drag him into this family mess. I'm curious how your father will handle this onslaught. As you know I haven't had any contact with him for so long. I think the last time was on the day we got divorced. I really don't know if he's the same man that I once knew and despised.'

'We'll soon find out.'

I am genuinely pleased that Mum is coming today. She's had a tough life. Dealing with a cruel and unfaithful husband and bringing up a challenging autistic child would have destroyed most people but not my mother. She has expressed her deep regrets many times over how she treated me but knowing what she went through I have come to terms with it and no longer feel any anger towards her. In fact I admire her so much for wanting to always do the best for Kieran. She has brought up my brother with no help. It's only been since Sienna has taken over the carer role that Mum was able to step back a bit. Sienna has helped to stabilise Kieran's behaviour and that's taken a lot of the pressure off my mother.

Although I still feel nervous, some of that anxiety has diminished knowing that my mother will be with us.

Shortly before ten o'clock we head out to Bournemouth. Mum is alongside me at the front of the car whilst Kieran and Sienna are at the back.

'I don't want to listen to that prick for two hours and thirty-two minutes,' Kieran tells me.

'Are you talking about the Sat Nav?' I ask.

'Yeah, the bloke whose talking through his arse. Just drive to Bournemouth. We don't need his bullshit.'

I'm relieved that he wasn't referring to me. I do what I'm told and switch off the Sat Nav.

Sienna takes out Kieran's portable DVD player and puts on one of his Bob Denny DVDs. Luckily Kieran's wearing headphones so all we hear is Kieran's laughter every few minutes, with occasional booing, which is all considerably better than Denny's infantile jokes.

'Thanks for coming along, Sienna. Strength in numbers and all that,' I say.

'If I'm honest I do feel a bit awkward. What if I just stay in the car when we arrive at your father's and you can call me if I'm needed.'

'I'd prefer it if you came in just in case Kieran kicks off. It'll be so much easier if you're with us but of course it's up to you.'

'Don't put any pressure on her,' my mother gently tells me.

'What if the old man is stringing us along and Kieran freaks out. My father's getting on a bit and when all is said and done I don't want Kieran attacking him.'

'OK, you've made your point, I'll go in with you,' Sienna replies, smiling.

'Thanks. We don't intend to stay long, just collect our dosh, slag him off and get the hell out of there.'

We spend most of the car journey in silence. Sienna tried to keep our spirits up but gave up when she got little response. The only person seemingly unaffected is Kieran who spends most of the journey laughing. Let's hope that mood continues during and after our stay.

We find the house without any help from Sat Nav. It's a small terraced house in a quiet street, not far from the beach. We wait in silence for a few minutes, half expecting my father to come out to greet us but that doesn't happen.

'OK, are we ready?' I finally say.

'Yeah, let's get this over and done with,' my mother replies.

We nervously walk up his driveway and ring the doorbell. A lady answers it straight away.

'Hello, I'm Helen, please come in,' she cheerfully tells us.

It's a friendly, if unexpected, welcome but my initial thoughts are why didn't he come out to greet us.

'Did you have any problems finding us?' She asks as she takes our coats.

'No, although Kieran didn't want to hear the Sat Nav chap giving us instructions so we switched it off,' I say.

'I don't blame him.'

She guides us into the living-room and there sitting in his armchair is my father. Understandably he looks older, thinner, less hair, just more frail looking. Helen helps him up to his feet. He's obviously not in good health.

'Thanks for coming, I really do appreciate it,' he tells me and offers his hand but I don't accept it. He doesn't react to my rejection.

'Hello, Sally, you're looking well,' he tells his ex-wife.

'I wish I could say the same about you. Are you OK?' She asks, looking anxious. The caring, loving side of my mother overrides the anger that she feels for her ex-husband.

'I had a stroke just before Christmas, I think my lifestyle from all those years ago has finally caught up with me.'

'George, why don't you sit down now?' Helen tells him.

'And let me introduce your other son, this is Kieran. He's the son that you don't give a fuck about. Fuck is a word that you're really familiar with, as during that time when you lived with us you were fucking around with as many women as you could get your grubby little hands on. I saw it for myself in a couple of pubs. You noticed me but you carried on fondling your female acquaintances, for want of a better word. I mean what sort of a person does that in front of their own son? Can you answer me that?' I ask my father.

He shakes his head but doesn't answer.

'And then you divulged all your sordid details to your wife. Did your stroke block all those memories?'

'OK, Ryan, I think you've said enough,' my mother tells me.

'Not yet. How do you live with yourself knowing that Kieran's autistic and you've never once showed him an ounce of affection? And when you finally did the decent thing and fucked off out of our lives you never once offered any financial or practical help to your wife, you just left her to get on with it. What have you got to say about that?'

I feel I'm ready to explode with anger right now.

'You're right in everything you've just said and no apology from me is going to make up for it, how could it? I should've reached out to you.'

'So why didn't you?'

'I know that this may sound pathetic but I didn't want to drag up all those awful memories for you all.'

'Yes, that does sound pathetic.'

'I was, and am, embarrassed and ashamed of my behaviour back then. I've often thought about everyone and…'

'But not enough to pick up a fucking phone to find out how we're getting on,' I interject.

Again my father doesn't react.

'When I left home I often wanted to find you and beat the fucking shit out of you. I didn't care of the consequences. Of course I can't do that now because you're an old man and barely alive but I wish I had. I wanted you to pay for what you did to us,' I shout at my father.

'OK, Ryan, stop it now,' my mother re-iterates.

'No, I won't,' I reply.

I approach him and stand inches away.

'So have you got anymore cliché excuses that you want to share with us?' I say to him.

He looks intently at me but then starts shaking. He looks unsteady but Helen grabs him and gently lays him back in his armchair.

'Are you OK, George? Shall I get you your medicine?' Helen asks.

'There's no need, I'm fine,' he says.

'Are you sure?'

He nods his reply.

'You went too far,' my mother tells me.

'No he didn't. I deserved it and so much more. Back then I wouldn't have cared about anything you had to say to me, but now I do, and I want to try and make it up to you all,' George replies.

I'm still so angry and want to respond but luckily I have enough presence of mind not to. I don't want to be responsible for causing any relapse, despite what I just told him.

'Where's my crisps?' Kieran asks, interrupting a pleasant father-son conversation.

My father gestures Helen to help him up again. He slowly walks towards my brother. Sienna then stands next to Kieran, ready to intervene.

'How are you son? You've grown into a handsome man,' he tells Kieran. I notice tears rolling his cheeks. 'I'm so sorry for everything.'

'You've forgotten my crisps, haven't you?' He says.

I stand on the other side of Kieran as this could escalate.

'On this occasion I haven't forgotten. Helen do you mind fetching Kieran's crisps?'

Helen smiles and leaves the living-room only to return a minute later carrying two boxes, she then brings in another two boxes.

'Thanks, Helen. That should keep you going for a while. There's all different flavours in there,' my father tells Kieran.

'You didn't put tomato ketchup crisps in any of those boxes?' Kieran asks.

My father looks at Helen.

'No, they're all pretty much the standard flavours. No weird ones,' Helen explains.

'But that's not fifteen years' worth is it?'

'No it isn't but here's some cash to help you buy as many as you like.'

He hands Kieran a wad of notes.

'How much is there?' I ask.

'Two and a half thousand pounds. Presumably you'll help him manage his spending?' He says, looking at me.

I don't respond.

'Wow, I'm rich. I don't have to work in that damn charity shop anymore. Was this the money you picked up when you worked as a whore?' He asks Helen.

'No, I've never actually worked…'

'Are you still a prostitute?' He asks before Helen can finish explaining.

My father smiles before Helen has a chance to respond.

'I've never been a prostitute. I worked as a dental assistant until three years ago when I retired,' she informs Kieran but he's already lost interest as he's just staring at his bank notes.

'George, why don't you sit down?' Helen asks her husband again but he shuffles towards my mother.

'I'm so sorry, Sally, for everything. I'm an utter shit for not contacting you then and now. What could I have said that would erase all those painful memories? Bringing up Kieran on your own must've have been so hard. I remember all too clearly you getting up night after night when Kieran wandered downstairs while I was sleeping off the inevitable hangover. Kieran was so difficult and I just couldn't handle it but you did even though I could see how much it took out of you. I'm ashamed that I didn't help in any way. As Ryan rightly pointed out the only decent thing I ever did was leave you but I should've helped you out financially. I was just too busy spending my money elsewhere. I hope that your life got better in some way after I left,' he tells my mother.

'I can't remember when I last had any love or affection for you. Maybe around the period when we got married but you soon put a stop to that by cheating on me a few weeks after our wedding day. Did you know how many times I literally cried myself to sleep, usually after you taunted me about your affairs? Most of my life I wished I'd never met you but you gave me Ryan and Kieran and that's the only positive thing to come out of our relationship. If it wasn't for the boys I would've ended my life because I was in utter despair nearly every single day of our marriage. But having said all of that I do forgive you because I know that you're genuinely sorry for everything. I'm convinced you mean what you're saying to us,' Mum replies.

My mother puts her arms around my father and hugs him. They're both crying.

I can't take any more of this and storm out of the house. Sienna follows me.

'What the fuck's going on in there?' I shout at Sienna.

'He's saying sorry and it looks like Sally's accepting that.'

'So for all those years of sheer torture that he heaped upon the whole family he's now trying to buy Kieran's affection with cash and crisps and a few mumbled apologies to Mum and everything's OK?'

'Ryan, as I've said to you earlier this is a personal family matter so it's entirely up to you what you do from here on in.'

'But you're always the voice of reason and being an outsider you can look at this from an objective point of view, so please tell what you think, you know I value your opinion.'

'I perfectly understand why you're upset but like Sally said I think you went too far. There's no doubt your father was a sadistic, inhumane and heartless man but what I saw in that living-room was an old, frail man who is apologising for all his transgressions. Would he have contacted any of you before you rang him last week? I doubt it but I do feel that he wants to make it up to you all and for me the only way forward is to accept his apology and move on. What's the alternative? Continuing to feel bitter towards him for the rest of your life? And how much longer does he have left?

Hopefully his health will improve but what will you think when he eventually does pass away and you didn't accept his apology? That might eat away at you or maybe it won't. Don't get me wrong I totally get why you can't forgive him, I really do but you don't have to be his best friend, just maybe try to be more civil towards him and draw a line under it. Take the crisps and dosh and drive back to Kings Cross. Kieran's happy and although Sally told him some harsh facts about his behaviour, she's forgiven him. I've said my peace. I better get inside to be with your brother.'

'Oh, Sienna, you really are the voice of reason,' I tell her.

I'm desperate to hug her but I refrain. There's to be no bodily contact until we hear from HR. She doesn't make any attempts to hug me so I'm assuming she feels the same. We make our way back to my father's house.

'I'm guessing you're Kieran's carer,' my father asks Sienna.

'Yes, I've been with him just over three years now.'

'Thank you for taking care of my son.'

'You're more than welcome. He's a lovely man.'

We all look at Kieran who is sitting on the sofa counting his money.

'Sienna's done incredible work with Kieran. I'd go as far to say that she's completely turned his life around for the better,' my mother tells her ex-husband.

'Yes, I can see that,' he replies, smiling.

'Look, Dad, I'll be honest with you. I can't forgive you as easily as Mum but I can see you're truly sorry for everything so let's just agree to move on. I appreciate your gifts to Kieran. As you can see he's delighted to receive that money and those crisp boxes will keep him quiet for a while because he's been banging on about them all week.'

He offers his hand again but instead of shaking it I engulf him in an embrace. We hold each other tightly for several minutes without saying anything and when we eventually step away Helen hands us both tissues to wipe away our tears.

I never expected that to happen.

CHAPTER THIRTY EIGHT: RYAN

Yesterday has got to be one of the most bizarre days of my life. The intense anger I felt walking up my father's driveway was similar to my feelings just before I first met Mum again and unbelievably the outcome from both of the encounters was pretty much the same.

It was only after chatting to Sienna outside the house that I began to see the bigger picture but to break down in tears only a few minutes later with my father in my arms just beggars belief.

We stayed for about an hour and my father even told us that he had included the three of us in his will a few months ago, before his stroke. This clearly shows he's a changed man. We made a promise to each other to keep in touch.

My mother looked relieved when we left, almost as if a great weight had just been lifted off her shoulders. It made such a welcome change to see how relaxed she appeared as normally she wears a permanent worried expression.

We were all extremely impressed with Helen. She's such a lovely woman who obviously cares deeply for my father. It was also nice to get the official confirmation and that she isn't, and never was, a lady of the night.

I'm standing at the entrance to Finsbury Park awaiting Kieran and Sienna. To try to erase the bad memory of our last visit here I suggested we repeat that same walk through the park but this time with just my brother. I'm wearing my usual shoulder and shin pads in addition to a scarf. I'm not sure how much the scarf would protect my neck from another attack but it's better than nothing.

As I'm waiting I reflect on the day when Sienna rang my front door bell for the first time. I was a little put out that she didn't give me any warning of her visit but she didn't have any contact number for me and wasn't even sure if my address was the right one. I was initially worried that something had happened to Kieran but when she reassured me that wasn't the case I more or less shut the door in her face. However things changed when she posted the photos of Kieran through the letter box. I was startled to see my brother as an adult for the first time. It was yet another ingenious Sienna manoeuvre.

It took much persuasion to orchestrate the meeting with my mother but I'm so glad that Sienna persisted. And of course meeting Kieran again was a life changing moment for me. Although the first two meetings with my brother didn't go well I'm beginning to see our relationship evolve. Once again this was predicted by Sienna. I need more time alone with him, without Abba, Steps or Black Lace drowning out our conversations and today I will have that opportunity. Once they arrive Sienna will leave and after our walk I will drop Kieran back at StarLight.

Of course the most unexpected reunion of all happened yesterday. I can't get over how well that all went. I still think I made the right decision in telling my father what I felt about his past behaviour and he didn't dispute one single point I made. Like Mum I just feel a great sense of relief. Subconsciously I've been carrying the burden of my traumatic childhood with me most of my life so to be on good terms with my parents and brother is just an unbelievable feeling.

I can see Sienna and Kieran walking towards me. Even though Kieran is a twenty-seven-year-old man Sienna still holds his hand crossing the road. As Sienna has told me many times road safety is not something he's interested in. I will have to make sure he's safe on the walk back to StarLight. In Kieran's other hand is a torch.

'Hi ya, how are you both doing today?' I ask as they approach me.

'We're OK, aren't we, Kieran?' Sienna replies.

Kieran is looking at his watch. We arranged to meet at two and it's now six minutes to two so he can't complain this time.

'I need to look at your ears,' he tells me. 'I tried doing that at the disco but it was too dark and that Black Lace song was distracting.'

'OK, go ahead,' I reply.

I anticipated this inspection, so true to my word I revisited the hairdressers and Matteo removed what little hairs there were in my ears and knowing this examination was imminent I've been keeping a close on the hair growth in that area ever since. Maybe I'm not that different from my brother after all?

Using his torch Kieran spends a couple of minutes studying each ear. My brother is very thorough when need be.

'That Matteo geezer has done a fantastic job, can you give me his number? I want to book an ear hair appointment. That guy should be on *Mastermind*,' Kieran tells me.

'My favourite subject, Clive, is ear hair growth.'

'Let me know when you want to go and I'll book an appointment for you,' I tell my brother.

He smiles back at me which is a rarity.

'Kieran do you mind if I have a quick word with Ryan in private?' Sienna asks.

'Is it about my ear hair appointment?'

'No, it's nothing to do with that.'

'OK, but make it quick, I'm busy,' he replies.

Oh yes, I forgot he's going to sort out an issue in the Middle East before having his dinner tonight.

Sienna pulls me to one side.

'What's up?' I ask.

'I've got a reply from HR, it's been in my spam folder for the last week.'

'And?'

'They've said it's not an issue unless Debbie objected. I've just had another chat with her and she's OK with it. We knew that anyway.'

'That's the best news ever. What the hell's happening here? Being reunited with my whole family and finally being able to go on an official date with you.'

'Not bad, eh.'

'Slight understatement. So where do you want to go on our first date?'

'We've already arranged to go to Brighton on Saturday, haven't we?'

'Of course. To be honest with everything else going on it just slipped my mind.'

She takes my hand and smiles at me.

'Are we staying overnight?' I ask.

'Yes, why not?'

'Wow, that's a bit forward of you.'

'We do have a lot of catching up to do.'

I lean forward to kiss her but she resists.

'Sorry, but we have to be careful around Kieran. In time that'll change.'

'Of course, I should've thought about that.'

'Look, I'm going to make my way back now. How about we bring forward our first date to tonight? Do you fancy going for a drink?'

'That's the most stupid question you've ever asked me and believe me you've asked me hundreds of questions during our short time together. The answer is yes,' I tell her.

We walk towards Kieran.

'Enjoy your time with your brother and I'll see you back at StarLight,' Sienna tells Kieran before leaving us.

'How long is this walk going to take?' Kieran asks.

'It's as short or as long as you want it to be,' I reply.

'OK, I want to get back to watch *Tipping Point* at three. I like Ben Shephard, he calms me down.'

'OK, we'll definitely be back to see Ben.'

The first few minutes of our walk is spent in silence. I'm waiting for him to instigate the conversation but that doesn't look like happening. My mind is still with Sienna, I can't believe that we can go out with each other without Big Brother looking over us. I've got to know her really well over the past couple of months and I'm absolutely convinced that we're in it for the long haul. I've never felt this way about anyone in my life. How Kieran will deal with this we'll have to wait and see but judging from every decision Sienna has made so far I'm confident she will have the right strategy at the right time to mitigate any possible issues.

This period of silence between Kieran and myself is a marked improvement on our previous time here as then he was walking a few hundred feet ahead of me and he reacted aggressively to everything I said to him. Again my mother's expression comes to mind – 'he'll eat the head off ya.' Hopefully that won't be the case today.

'Did you enjoy your visit to Bournemouth?' I ask.

'It was fantastic to get all those bank notes. There was one thousand pounds in fifty pound notes, one thousand pounds in twenty pound notes, four hundred pounds in ten pound notes and one hundred pounds in five pound notes. They were all very crisp, which made it difficult to count as they kept sticking together. I wished he got a mixture of old and new ones. I'll write him a letter about that. I wanted to carry the two thousand and five hundred pounds out with me today but Sienna told me to just bring twenty so I decided to put a ten and two five pounds in my wallet.'

'That was very generous of Dad to give you that, wasn't it?'

'Will he give me another two thousand five hundred pounds the next time I visit?'

'No, that was a one off.'

'So is he going to turn into a bastard again?'

'No, he won't.'

It's interesting that he referred to him as a bastard. Despite his autism he must have still realised that he wasn't a good person.

'What are you going to spend your money on?' I ask.

'Crisps.'

'Why don't you hold off buying some more until you've gone through the four boxes?'

'Oh, OK, but I hope the shops will still be selling them,' he replies.

'Rest assured they will.'

A few weeks ago he would have got annoyed at any of my suggestions; it's progress.

'He wasn't wearing his white t-shirt and kept on crying. Was that because he couldn't find his white t-shirt?'

'No, he was crying because he was emotional seeing everyone again,' I respond.

'But why does that make him emotional?'

'He hadn't seen his family for so long and I think he was just sad and happy at the same time.'

'But that was all his own fault.'

'I know but still…'

Again I'm surprised that he knew that it was Dad's fault that he hadn't seen us for fifteen years if that's what he meant.

'You didn't cry when I first saw you at the restaurant. Was that because you were just interested in eating your pizza?' Kieran asks me.

'No, I was much more interested in seeing you again. Emotion affects people in different ways.'

'It's confusing,' he replies.

It certainly is.

'Can I ask you a favour, Kieran?'

He looks at me but doesn't respond.

'Can I now let my hair grow back and not dye it?'

'No, that'll put my brain into a bad mood.'

'OK, that's no problem. I'll keep it short so you see my ears and forehead and I won't let any grey hairs creep in.'

He doesn't acknowledge this life-long commitment that I'm undertaking.

'Did you ever think about me after I left home?' I ask.

'Yes I did. I remember you leaving but I thought you were coming back, so every day I looked out onto the street wondering where you'd gone or did you just get lost. Mum kept telling me that you moved into a new house but I thought she was lying.'

I wonder why Mum never told me that? Probably to protect me from feeling even more guilty.

'We're back together now, aren't we?' I say.

'Yes, but will you get lost again?'

No, that's never going to happen. In fact can I ask you for another favour?'

He doesn't acknowledge me but instead is staring at his watch. Not missing Ben Shephard is obviously more important than anything I've got to say.

'Can I hug you?' I ask.

'And how are you going to do that?' He replies.

'I'd like to put my arms around you, if that's OK?'

'What's the point of that?'

'It's just a sign of affection.'

'And what do I do?'

'Your choice. You can just stand there and do nothing or you can put your arms around me.'

'I'm just going to stand still,' he tells me.

I gently embrace my brother. He doesn't resist.

'I love you,' I whisper to him.

I hold him for a minute or so and just as I'm about to step away he reciprocates.

I look over Kieran's shoulder and a few feet away is the same man who was on the verge of calling the police after Kieran attacked me the last time we were here. He's walking his dog again. I wave to him and he smiles back. A lot has changed since that day. The most important change is I've got my brother back in my life and I'm going to keep on reassuring him that I'm never going to leave him ever again.

THE END

Milton Keynes UK
Ingram Content Group UK Ltd.
UKHW011304210923
429112UK00001B/18